This book must be returned by the date specified at the time of issue as
the DATE DUE FOR RETURN.
The loan may be extended (personally, by post, telephone or online) for
a further period if the book is not required by another reader, by quoting
the above number / author / title.   **2 4 DEC 2019**

DISTRACTED
BY HER VIRTUE

DISTRACTED
BY HER VIRTUE

BY

MAGGIE COX

First published in Great Britain 2012
by Mills & Boon, an imprint of Harlequin (UK) Limited.
Large Print edition 2012
Harlequin (UK) Limited, Eton House,
18-24 Paradise Road, Richmond, Surrey TW9 1SR

© Maggie Cox 2012

ISBN: 978 0 263 23655 2

Harlequin (UK) policy is to use papers that are natural, renewable and recyclable products and made from wood grown in sustainable forests. The logging and manufacturing process conform to the legal environmental regulations of the country of origin.

Printed and bound in Great Britain
by CPI Antony Rowe, Chippenham, Wiltshire

To Lesley, who never fails to make me laugh
and see the funny side of things!

You are such a blessing
and I'm so glad that we're friends.

CHAPTER ONE

As JARRETT picked his way carefully down the steep grassy bank that was made potentially treacherous by the odd jagged stone hidden amongst the greenery the chocolate-brown Lab accompanying him passed him with a swift, much more sure-footed tread. He lifted his head to follow the dog's enthusiastic trail, and his gaze was suddenly captured by an unexpected sight. At the foot of the valley just ahead, down by the familiar babbling brook that the dog usually made a beeline for, he spied the unfamiliar figure of a lithe young woman dressed in jeans and a khaki-coloured weatherproof jacket. Her hands held a camera, and as he observed her she dropped to her haunches to photograph something.

At this distance it was hard to see what it was,

but it crossed Jarrett's mind that the woman might be one of those horticulturists who occasionally visited the area, cataloguing some rare plant or flower. It was a fine spring day and, having just closed the deal on a prime parcel of land not twenty miles from here, Jarrett was predisposed to be sociable.

'Hello there!' he called out as he drew nearer, and the woman lifted her head and glanced round at him, startled. As he drew nearer, the beauty of her face literally stopped him in his tracks. *Who was she?* Inside his chest his heart thumped hard—as though he'd sprinted down that treacherous hillside. He'd never come across eyes of such a light green hue before…like the softest summer grass. And the silky mantle of chestnut hair that flowed down over her shoulders was the perfect foil to bring out the colour, he thought with pleasure as his lips formed an appreciative smile. 'It's a beautiful day, isn't it?'

'Charlie? Charlie, come over here to me right now!'

He hadn't seen the child, but at the woman's

urgent-voiced command, like an arrow expertly released from its bow to fly towards its target, he appeared out of a distant clump of trees and threw himself into her lap, almost knocking her over. *Was she his mother?* Jarrett wondered. She looked almost too young.

Though she might just be a passing stranger, the need to know who she was wouldn't leave him alone. 'I didn't mean to startle you,' he apologised, holding out his hand, 'My name's Jarrett Gaskill. I live on the other side of that rise up there.'

If he'd been expecting her to reciprocate with similar information then he was doomed to disappointment. Glancing at his outstretched hand, the green-eyed beauty made no move to take it. Instead she laid down her camera, sat back on the grass and tenderly patted the small boy on his back, as if to reassure him that everything was all right. The child's riot of dark curls was tucked beneath her chin as if he wanted to hide.

'I know it may not look like it, but I'm not taking pictures purely for my own amusement. I'm actually working.'

The bewitching green eyes flashed, but for a moment Jarrett's attention was more captivated by her voice. There was such resolve and firmness in its husky tones—a *warning* too—that it took him aback. *Did she think he presented some kind of threat to her and the child?*

The thought made him retreat a couple of steps, and he let his hand drop uselessly down by his side. As if to remind him of his presence, the chocolate Lab that he was dog-sitting for his sister Beth nudged his muzzle into his palm and gave him a lick. The creature had done his usual trick of galloping joyfully through the water, and as a result was now sopping wet from head to tail. 'It's all right, boy…we'll be on our way in just a minute.'

'Was there something else?'

The woman appeared almost affronted that he might be contemplating staying for even a second longer when she'd clearly demonstrated that his presence wasn't welcome. Swallowing down the disagreeable sense of rejection that curdled briefly in the pit of his stomach, Jarrett met her unflinching glare with an equally unwavering one of his own. His lip even curled a little mockingly. 'No…I was simply passing the time of day. Nothing more sinister than that.'

'Don't be offended. It's just that when I'm working I have to give my full attention to my subject. If I allow myself to get distracted then the photograph turns out to be useless.'

'In that case I won't distract or disturb you any longer. Enjoy the rest of your day.'

'You too.'

'Come on, Dylan…time for us to go.'

The boy on her lap turned his head to steal a helpless glance of longing at the dog. Jarrett saw that the child, too, was uncommonly striking. But his bright long-lashed eyes weren't the arresting green of the woman's. They were a dark berry-brown. *Was* she his mother? he wondered again. He'd love to know. More to the point, did she come from one of the nearby villages? Due to the demands of his business, he didn't spend a lot of time at home, but nonetheless he didn't think she was a native of the area. *He was certain he would have heard about her if she was.* Such beauty would not go unnoticed for long.

Despite his curiosity, Jarrett knew that it was time for him to go. As he turned away it felt as if the bright day had suddenly dimmed. Even the memory of the deal he had just closed couldn't diminish the blow to his ego that the green-eyed beauty had dealt him with her indifference and distrust.

'Her name's Sophia Markham. She's moved into High Ridge Hall.'

'What?' The information his sister had so helpfully provided when she'd rung to let him know that she and her husband Paul had returned from their weekend trip to Paris had sent a thunderbolt jack-knifing through Jarrett's heart. He'd been trying to purchase the old manor house for years, but the elderly lady who had lived there until two Christmases ago had doggedly refused to sell—even when it became clear that the building was heading for rack and ruin due to her neglect. The place had been standing empty since she'd died, and even though he'd made several enquiries to all the local agencies neither they nor he were any the wiser regarding who owned it or what was going to happen to it now. So now, when Beth so matter-of-factly told him that the girl he'd described down by the stream yesterday had moved into it he was crushed with disappointment.

High Ridge Hall was much more than just a once grand crumbling edifice he yearned to restore to its former glory. Historically, it had always been the seat of one of the richest families in the area. Owning such a place would set the seal on the successes of the past few years during which his 'property empire'—as Beth teasingly called it—had gone from strength to strength. He couldn't help but feel jealous that the green-eyed beauty had moved into the place. She must have some important connections indeed for her to be able to live there—even though it must be falling down round her ears. But then, as he remembered the powerful tug of attraction he'd experienced towards her almost on sight, he was reminded of the lustful heat that had assailed him at just a single glance from her bewitching eyes…

'Local opinion is that she is related to old Miss Wingham,' said Beth. 'How else could she move in? The place wasn't even put up for sale.'

'Damn it all to hell!'

'Mum would turn in her grave if she heard you say that, Jarrett.'

'Thankfully I'm not encumbered by our late mother's religious proclivities—and nor should you be,' he answered irritably.

'Anyway…you say you met her down by the stream in the valley? I hear she has a son. Was he with her?'

'Yes. He was.'

'There's no evidence of a father or husband. Do you think she's divorced? Or maybe her husband works abroad?'

'You're becoming as nosey as the rest of the village.'

'Don't pretend you're not interested. I hear our Ms Markham is a real looker.'

Jarrett elected not to reply. He was still coming to terms with the idea that purchasing the house—a goal he had set his heart on—was no longer an option. At the other end of the line his sister emitted a long-suffering sigh.

'Couple that with the fact that she's moved into High Ridge Hall, and my guess is that you won't be so eager to fly off on any long-haul business trips any time soon…at least not until you find out how she got the house and who she is.'

'Well, you're wrong about that. As a matter of fact I'm flying out to New York on Friday. I expect to be away for at last a fortnight, if not more.'

'I'm only teasing you, little brother.'

'Don't call me that,' replied Jarrett, who at six foot two could scarcely be described as 'little'.

'To me you'll always be my little brother. And with both our parents gone it's down to me to keep a sisterly eye on you. Changing the subject—have you seen anything of Katie Stewart lately?'

Katie Stewart? The woman he'd taken out on

a few dates he hadn't even wanted to go on? She had barely crossed Jarrett's mind. Her company was pleasant enough, but her conversation hardly lit up the world. As attractive as she was, he wouldn't date any woman purely because she was easy on the eye. At the very least she had to be bright and engaging, with a good sense of humour. And of course the most important element of all was that there had to be some fundamental connection between them—an undeniable spark that would keep him interested. At thirty-six he was still single, and it wasn't hard to understand why. The kind of woman his heart secretly yearned for seemed hard to find—at least in *his* world. Beth put it down to pickiness, but Jarrett preferred to consider himself discerning.

'No, I haven't seen Katie Stewart lately. When and *if* I do I'll be sure to give you a report.'

'I just worry about you having no one who really matters to you in your life. All the money and success in the world won't make you happy or keep you warm on those bitter winter nights, Jarrett.'

He grinned into the receiver. 'Now you're sounding like one of those batty psychics that tell you you're going to meet a tall dark stranger if you cross their palm with silver.'

'Is Sophia Markham tall?'

Jarrett's grin immediately turned into a scowl. 'I've no idea. When I saw her she was crouching to take a photograph. Anyway, I've got to get on. I'll bring the dog back to you around lunchtime, shall I?'

'Are you angling for a lunch invitation?'

'Throw a slice of ham between a couple of slices of bread, make me a cup of tea and I won't dash off. I'll stay and have a chat with you.'

'The day I "throw" a slice of ham between two slices of bread and call it lunch, I'll know I've seriously lost the plot!'

Reflecting on some of the wonderful meals his sister had made for him long before she'd gone to catering college and eventually become head chef for one of the high-end restaurants in the west end of London, Jarrett's feelings towards Beth palpably softened. 'You're a true culinary genius, sweetheart, and believe me—both my stomach and my palate are grateful for it. I'll see your around one o'clock, shall I?'

'And don't forget to bring Dylan with you, will you?'

'As if I'd forget… Every time I turn round he's either doing his best to enslave me with those huge seal-pup eyes of his or trip me over!'

As she drew back the ancient tapestry drapes, the rain of dust made Sophia cough violently. She stepped back just in time as the heavy brass curtain rail clattered heavily down onto the dark wooden floor.

'Of all the stupid things to do…' she muttered.

Knowing she'd had a lucky escape, she shook her head, planted her hands on her hips and smiled ruefully. For a while she just stood, watching the dust motes that jumped up from the floor swirl madly in the beam of sunlight that arrowed in through the window. If she'd longed for a project to help quell the misery and despair of the past then she'd found one right enough. It was going to take a good deal of hard toil, sweat and probably tears too to make this house any*where near* comfortable enough to enjoy living in. But she hardly had cause for complaint. Not when her eccentric Great-Aunt Mary had bequeathed her such an incredible gift.

Who would have guessed that a woman who had barely even acknowledged her as a child except to frown down at her through her half-moon glasses would turn out to be her guardian angel and fairy godmother all rolled into one?

'Aunt Mary dislikes most of her family...the adults at any rate,' Sophia's dad had told her once, even as his merry green eyes twinkled mischievously. 'She doesn't believe that we deserve to count her as a relative. We're a great disappointment to her, I'm sure. When she goes she'll leave this gothic monstrosity of a house to some cat or dog charity...just wait and see!'

Well...her eccentric great-aunt *hadn't* bequeathed High Ridge Hall to an animal charity. *She'd left it to Sophia instead.*

The day before she'd been due to leave the

home that she had been forced to sell she'd had a phone call from a solicitor's office in London. They had spent months trying to track her down, to tell her that she was the sole beneficiary in her great-aunt's will. Sophia had been appalled—she hadn't even heard that she'd died. Since her dad had passed away she'd lost touch with practically everyone but her brother David, and she saw him infrequently enough. In a way she was glad. Since her husband's destructive behaviour and alcoholism had grown even worse, she'd become too ashamed to let family or friends see how low she had sunk. To learn that not only had she been left High Ridge Hall but a small amount of money too had been overwhelming.

Dropping down into the one remaining antique chair in the living room that hadn't yet been sold to help meet her deceased husband's mountain of debt, Sophia had cried hard with gratitude and relief at her eleventh-hour reprieve. If her great-aunt hadn't left her beautiful old house to her even contemplating the alternative living arrangements insisted upon by her bullying father-in-law would have been too grim to bear...

Her little son ran in from the kitchen, his dark eyes round as saucers when he saw the dislodged brass rail and the pile of old curtains that half smothered it. 'What happened, Mummy? I heard the loudest bang.'

'The curtain rail fell down. These walls are very old, Charlie. The plaster is crumbling like powder. It's going to take a lot of work to make this room nice again... The whole house is in need of some major attention to make it fit to live in. I'm only grateful that your uncle David was able to take some time off to get a couple of the rooms ready for us before we moved in—otherwise we would have had to camp out in the garden in a tent!'

Charlie was already losing interest in the dramatic incident that had caused him to rush in from the kitchen. Instead he was staring down at the colourful toy he'd carried into the room with him, restlessly turning it over and over between his fingers, as if itching to employ it in some way.

'Can I go out to the garden to play? I want to make a fort. I promise I won't go near the pond.'

'All right, then. As long as you keep in full view of these windows so that I can see you. Promise?'

He grinned, showing a couple of gaps where he'd lost his baby teeth.

Sophia's heart squeezed. 'Give me a hug and a kiss first.'

'You're *always* hugging and kissing me.'

'I know, but I can't help it!' Seizing her young son by the waist, she whirled him round and round until he shrieked with laughter.

'Let me go!' he begged. 'You're making me dizzy!'

When he'd got his bearings again, he threw his mother a disarming grin and rushed out of the house into the wild forest of a garden—the garden that was already keeping Sophia awake at night, as she planned how she was going to make it beautiful again and restore it to the fairytale garden of her childhood.

As she bent down to retrieve the curtains and

the rail, out of the blue an image stole into her mind of the physically arresting man who had stopped to say hello the other day while she'd been taking photographs of wildflowers for her portfolio. His eyes had been electrifyingly blue, yet his hair was a thick, curling cap of ebony silk. A small flare of heat imploded inside her. Despite her attraction to him Sophia had been nervous. *What if her father-in-law had sent him to find her... to force her to return to the neighbourhood where she had lived with her late husband?*

God knew the man had the kind of strong, intimidating physique that could easily overwhelm her if he tried. She inhaled a long steadying breath. Her worst fears thankfully hadn't come true, but she was still uneasy.

Jarrett Gaskill...what kind of a name was that?

Even if the man had never heard of her illustrious father-in-law, his name sounded a little too highbrow and pompous for her taste. No doubt he was some ambitious city type who kept a second home here in the country for weekends where he could entertain his London friends and play Lord of the Manor.

The thought brought a briefly cynical smile to her lips, before making her frown. Remembering his mellifluous tones, she'd thought he'd sounded sincere enough. Perhaps it was wrong of her to so judge him so quickly. But what did she know of sincere men when she'd been married to the biggest liar and cheat in the country? Tom Abingdon—the man she'd so stupidly rushed headlong into marriage with at eighteen against all advice—had been cruel, possessive, and self-indulgent to excess, as well as vain and self-obsessed, and the signs had been there right from the beginning.

How incredible, how *naive*, that Sophia had once believed she could turn him away from his destructive tendencies and show him that life together could be good. It hadn't taken her long to find out how contemptuous he was of her sincere and innocent impulses. The dark road she'd been travelling with him had grown darker and more twisted day by day, and somehow, because her spirits had sunk so low, she'd been unable to find any means of breaking free.

Towards the end of his life he'd been intent on dragging her and their small son down to even more despicable lows, until one day, in the midst of her growing despair, it had suddenly become clear to her that she had to abandon her youthful dreams of 'happy-ever-after'—she couldn't fix her self-destructive husband's life and she should walk away…right *now*. For Charlie's sake, if not her own.

It was that thought that had rejuvenated hope in her—had spurred her on to make plans to leave him. But fate had had other more finite plans for Tom Abingdon. One night, after a heavy bout of drinking, he'd died in his sleep.

For a few unsteadying moments the sickening hurt and fury at the pain he had caused deluged Sophia's heart and made her suck in her breath. Perhaps it was an apt reminder of the supreme idiocy of her getting involved with anyone ever again. If Tom was anything to go by, it was all too easy to be mesmerised and trapped by a man.

Even the liars and cheats of this world could present a normal façade in order to get what they wanted, and it made her vow to be extra careful and much more vigilant.

If she ever saw him again, she promised herself she would give Jarrett Gaskill a wide berth. There was no way she would give *any* man the opportunity to get to know her…to discover the shameful truth of her marriage to a man who had frequently mistreated and degraded her. A new beginning was what she wanted for her and her son. One that didn't include strangers—however friendly—who wanted to pry into her business. Not that she kidded herself for an instant that Jarrett Gaskill would even remember bumping into her and Charlie down by that idyllic little brook.

For the past three weeks Sophia had visited the weekly farmers' market in the town centre. There was nothing like buying fruit and vegetables straight from the source, rather than from a soulless and anodyne supermarket, she thought.

It was fresher, smelled better, and the taste far surpassed anything you could buy packaged and wrapped up in plastic.

Drawing her son closer to her side, she accepted the sturdy brown paper bag of apples she'd just bought from a friendly female stallholder and deposited it into her hessian shopping bag, on top of the other fresh produce she'd purchased. Glancing down at the cherubic little face that gazed up at her, she smiled brightly in anticipation of her plans for the afternoon. It was still such a treat to bake pies and cakes without fear of Tom coming home drunk, mocking her efforts and then throwing them against the wall.

'We'll make an apple pie to have with our tea tonight, Charlie,' she promised cheerfully.

'You don't want an extra guest, do you? I'm quite partial to home-made apple pie.'

The arresting male voice was so richly resonant and well-spoken that Sophia glanced up in surprise at the man who had stepped up beside her. Her startled gaze was instantly magnetised by a pair of twinkling blue eyes so rivetingly intense that for a moment she couldn't speak. It was *him*...Jarrett Gaskill. The name that had been warily filed away inside her brain presented itself with worrying ease.

'No...I don't. I've not long moved into my house and it's taking me longer than I expected to get settled. Besides, it's not likely I'd invite someone into my home that I don't even know,' she replied, quickly averting her gaze.

'I told you my name the first time we met, remember?'

Sophia's cheeks burned with heat, because she wasn't able to pretend that she couldn't recall it. 'That's neither here nor there. Knowing a person's name hardly means that you *know* them.'

'True...but an introduction at least creates the opportunity to *get* to know someone.'

'I'm sorry, Mr Gaskill, but I really must get on.'

'You see?' Something akin to delight was mirrored in the azure depths of his compelling glance. 'You *did* remember my name. Perhaps now you'll do me the honour of telling me yours?'

'I don't think so.' Already turning away, Sophia

was suddenly eager to leave the busy little market that was set up in the picturesque village square and head for home.

'What a pity. I've got to call you something if we bump into each other again, don't you think?'

'No, you don't. You can simply ignore me.'

His strong brow affected an exaggerated frown. 'I certainly couldn't. That would be the height of bad manners.'

'You really care about things like good manners?'

'Of course. I'd live in dread of my poor deceased mother haunting me if I didn't keep her standards up.'

In spite of her eagerness to extricate herself from this unwanted and surreal conversation, Sophia couldn't suppress a smile. But almost as soon as she'd succumbed to the gesture she firmed her lips into a much more serious line. 'I've really got to go. I've got things to do. Goodbye.'

Firmly tightening her hold on her son's small hand, she was about to walk out into the milling throng exploring the market stalls when the man standing beside her spoke clearly.

'Enjoy that apple pie, Ms Markham…perhaps you'll save me a slice?'

She spun round, her eyes widening in alarm. 'Who told you my name?'

'You've moved into a village…sooner or later everyone learns the name of a newcomer. They also tend to speculate on where they've come from and why they've moved here. Human nature, I guess.'

He shrugged nonchalantly, and Sophia stared. It was hard to ignore the width of those broad, well-defined shoulders beneath his well-worn, expensive-looking leather jacket. The black T-shirt he wore underneath with jeans was stretched across an equally well-defined chest, and he exuded the kind of masculine strength that made her even more wary of him. But more than that she was uncomfortable with the fact that people she didn't even know might be discussing her and her son.

'People should mind their own business! If my name should ever be mentioned in your hearing again, Mr Gaskill, I'd be obliged if you would make it very clear that I want to be left in peace.'

'I don't hold with gossiping about anyone. However, I will endeavour to respect your desire for privacy, Ms Markham.'

Sophia's glance was wary, but she made herself acknowledge his remark just the same. 'Thank you.'

Before Jarrett could engage her further, she took herself and Charlie off into the crowd and didn't once glance back to see if his disturbing blue gaze followed them…even though her heart thudded fit to burst inside her chest at the thought that he might indeed be following her progress…

CHAPTER TWO

CHARLIE was playing in the overgrown front garden as Jarrett drove his Range Rover up to the impressive old house. Glancing out of his window up at the pearlescent sky that threatened rain, he grimaced. Before he talked himself out of it he was on his feet, opening the creaking iron gate that led onto a meandering gravel path sprouting with weeds.

He stopped to talk to the child. 'Hello, there.' Jarrett smiled. 'Your name's Charlie, isn't it?'

'Where's your dog?'

Large dark eyes stared hopefully up at him. He was gratified that the boy seemed to remember him. It was two weeks since they'd last met. He also guessed that he probably didn't have a pet of his own. For some reason, that bothered him.

Dropping down to his haunches, so that he was

on the same level as the child, Jarrett frowned with genuine regret. 'I'm afraid that he doesn't belong to me. I was just looking after him for my sister. He's back with her now.'

'Oh.' His young companion was stumped for a moment. Recovering, he fixed his visitor with another interested gaze. 'You called him Dylan.'

'Yes, I did. That's his name.'

'It's a good name. But if I had a dog I'd call him Sam.'

'That's a good name too. Would you like a dog of your own?'

The boy studied him gravely. 'Yes, I would… But Mummy thinks a dog would be too much trouble to take care of—and we've had enough trouble already.'

Jarrett absorbed this very interesting snippet of information, ruffled the boy's unruly dark hair, then rose to his full height again. 'Never mind…perhaps in time she might have a change of heart?'

'No, she won't.' Charlie kicked a nearby pebble with the scuffed toe of his trainer, but not before giving Jarrett a look that said he wished she *could* be persuaded differently. 'Have you come to see her?' he asked.

'Yes, I have. Is she inside?'

'She's painting.'

Did Sophia Markham's creative talent extend beyond photography to painting?

Jarrett was still considering the idea as he strode up to the front door. The faded sandstone of the house reflected the more muted, mellow tones of a bygone age. The whole building was in dire need of some serious maintenance and re-decoration, but no one could deny it had tremen-dous potential and charm. If he owned the place he would know *exactly* which restoration com-pany to hire to help return it to its former glory.

Biting back his disappointment that he would now never have the chance, he made robust use of the heavy brass door-knocker and waited for Sophia to appear. He couldn't deny he was a lit-tle apprehensive about seeing the emerald-eyed beauty again. Both times that he'd tried to en-gage her in conversation she'd been decidedly aloof. He'd already received a warning that all she wanted to do was to be left in peace. And, despite his sister Beth and her friends still speculating on the whereabouts of a man in her life, Jarrett was becoming more and more convinced that, aside from her son, the mysterious Sophia was unattached.

'For goodness' sake, sweetheart, the back door is open. You don't need to—' Sophia bit off the comment that was clearly meant for Charlie and stared up in open-mouthed surprise at Jarrett. *'You!'* She shook her head as if to clear it, and her already loosened ponytail drifted free from its band, so that long silken strands of the glossiest chestnut-brown fell down over her shoulders. A faded pink T-shirt spattered with blue and white paint highlighted the small pert breasts underneath it, and a pair of slim-fitting denims with a large ragged hole in one knee clung to long, slender legs.

Jarrett raised an eyebrow. If she'd appeared in a couture dress from one of the top fashion houses in Paris he couldn't imagine her looking sexier than she did right then. Facing the pair of annoyed and sparkling green eyes that glared back at him, he couldn't deny the powerful surge of sexual heat that tumbled forcefully through him.

'How did you find out where I live?'

'The house has been empty for quite a while. Didn't you think that people would notice when it became occupied again?'

With what looked like a weary effort, she dragged her fingers through her loosened chestnut hair and shrugged. 'I get the feeling that people round here notice a little bit too much.'

'Anyway…my apologies for interrupting what looks like a very industrious Sunday afternoon for you. Your son said you were painting? Does that mean you're a painter as well as a photographer?'

'I'm painting my sitting room…not a canvas.'

'Okay.' He held up his hands, grinning at his mistake. 'At any rate, I dropped by because I have an invitation to give to you—from my sister, Beth.' He produced what was, in his opinion, a ridiculously scented and girly-pink envelope from the inside pocket of his three-quarter-length black leather jacket.

'Have I met your sister?'

Amusement forced one corner of Jarrett's mouth up into his cheek. 'Not yet...but, trust me, she's determined to meet *you*, Ms Markham—or is it Mrs?'

Her expression became even more vexed. She snatched the envelope from him. 'It's Ms. I used to be married, but I'm not any more.'

'So you're divorced?'

He saw her swallow hard. 'No. I'm a widow.'

The news sobered Jarrett's mood. 'I'm sorry.'

'Don't be. I'm *not*. And before you make some specious judgement about that, the topic isn't up for discussion.'

'Fair enough...that's your prerogative.'

The fire in her eyes suddenly died. Gripping the pink envelope he'd handed her as if she'd prefer to rip it to shreds rather than open it, she laid the flat of her free hand against the doorframe, as if needing support. It was as though every ounce of her vitality and strength had leaked away, leaving her visibly weak and shaken.

To be that *angry*…that *aloof*…must take a hell of a lot of energy, Jarrett mused. *What had the woman been through to make her so furious and defensive?* Her remark about not being sorry that she was a widow suggested that her relationship with her husband had not been the stuff of fairytales.

For whatever pain she'd endured in the past, a genuine feeling of compassion arose inside him. 'Ms Markham…Sophia…are you all right?'

'I'm fine.'

With a look of steely resolve she straightened, but he could hardly miss the tears that glistened in her eyes, and the sight made him feel as if he'd just been punched in the gut. He never *had* been able to bear seeing a woman cry…

'How did you know my name was Sophia?' she challenged.

Before Jarrett had the chance to answer, she folded her arms and wryly moved her head from side to side.

'I expect it filtered down to you from the head-quarters of the local gossip collective. Am I right?'

'I can't deny it.'

'Do people have such dull and boring lives that they have to pry into the business of a total stranger?' she demanded irritably.

'They most likely *do*. Why do you think they're so addicted to the soaps on TV? The invented drama of a stranger's life is probably far preferable to the reality of their own.'

'I won't have a TV in the house. I'd rather read a book.'

'What about Charlie?' Jarrett ventured, glancing over at the small boy who was once again careening round the giant hollyhocks, mimicking the 'rat-a-tat' sound of machine gun fire.

Sophia winced. 'My son doesn't need to be glued to a television or computer screen to enjoy himself. Besides, a lot of the programmes shown nowadays are so negative and manipulative that he's hardly missing out on anything helpful or essential.'

'So…what kind of books do you like to read?'

'If you're hoping that I'll invite you in to have a cup of tea and discuss my reading habits, then I'm sorry, Mr Gaskill, but I'm going to have to disappoint you. You may keep turning up like the proverbial bad penny, but I'm not going to encourage you.'

'You have something against making friends?'

'I manage just fine without them.'

'What about your son?'

'What *about* him?'

'You might prefer to be reclusive, but what about Charlie? Doesn't he need the companionship of children his own age?'

'He's joining the village primary school in a couple of weeks, so he'll make lots of friends there, I'm sure.'

'My sister Beth's best friend Molly teaches the nursery class. If you come to Beth's little get-together next Saturday you're bound to meet her. Who knows? You might even become friends.'

Sophia huffed out a sigh. 'What *is* it with you? Are you employed to go round the village encouraging fellowship amongst its inhabitants whether they want it or not?'

Jarrett laughed. To be honest, he couldn't remember the last time that a woman's witty repartee had engaged him quite so much—*thrilled* him, even. 'No, I'm not… Though it seems to me that would be a quite commendable way to spend my time. The downside is I could hardly earn a living doing it.'

Tapping the pink envelope against her thigh, Sophia gave an impatient glance that didn't reflect a similar enjoyment in his company. 'Look…I'm in the middle of decorating the sitting room and I must get on. I'm sorry if I seem a little terse, but I have my work cut out trying to make this place into a home for me and Charlie. Thanks for taking the time and trouble to bring me the invitation. You can tell your sister that I'll think about it and let her know.'

'If you do that much she'll be delighted, I'm sure.' He held out his hand without much hope or expectation that she would take it. He almost stumbled when she slid her cool palm inside his. It was as light and as delicate as a bird.

'Goodbye, Mr Gaskill.' She quickly withdrew it, but not before his skin tingled fiercely from its contact with hers.

'Now that we've introduced ourselves you can call me Jarrett. Goodbye…Sophia.' Before turning away he gave her a deliberately teasing smile, lifted his hand in a wave to Charlie, then strode back down the uneven path and out through the gate to his car…

Reflecting on her most recent encounter with Jarrett Gaskill disturbed Sophia so much that, despite her assertion that she had work to do, the desire to spend the rest of her Sunday afternoon painting the sitting room utterly deserted her. In search of a solution to the hard-to-contain restlessness his visit had left her with, she jumped with Charlie into the small second-hand car she'd recently purchased and drove down to the coast.

The spring day was chilly, but they still ate their fish and chips outside, sitting on a bench overlooking the foaming silver sea, and the gusting wind that blew around them was sufficiently cold to prevent Sophia from dwelling on any of the worries that were usually hovering just below the surface of her conscious thoughts.

When they'd finished eating, she bought her son a crabbing line from a nearby corner shop, along with some bacon to use for bait. Then they walked back down to the seafront, where they enjoyed a pleasantly distracting time fishing about in the murky shallows for baby crabs. After Charlie had diligently counted their catch, they conscientiously dropped them back into the water again.

On the journey home, her exuberant son fell fast asleep in his car seat, worn out by his afternoon's activities. At last Sophia could mull over the man who so persistently seemed to want to get to know her. *She didn't doubt that he had great ability to charm the ladies.* How could he not, with that carved handsome face, those flawless blue eyes and a voice that was mellifluous and compelling?

As she took the road out of the village that led almost straight to High Ridge Hall, she wondered why Jarrett would take the trouble to deliver an invitation to his sister's 'little get-together' by hand? Was it because he wanted to get a chance to look more closely at the house? The idea deflated her and she didn't know why. She knew that High Ridge had always held a fascination not just for local people but also for passing ramblers. The imposing early nineteenth-century edifice demanded more than just a fleeting glance. Her great-aunt had often had to contend with strangers knocking on the door to enquire after its history.

The idea of her elderly relative giving short shrift in response to those enquiries brought an instant smile to Sophia's lips. It also reminded her of the great responsibility of taking care of such a house. With the proceeds from the sale of the house she'd shared with her husband and a not insubstantial part of her inheritance from her aunt already gone to help pay off his debts, it was vital that she was able to revive the photographic career that had promised to take off when she'd left college. The career that when she'd had Charlie she'd foolishly and naively put aside, to be the stay-at-home wife and mother that her husband had demanded she be.

A residence the size and importance of High Ridge demanded that she earn a healthy income to maintain it. What little money that was left from her inheritance after all her outgoings were met wasn't going to last very long. Thankfully she'd kept a note of some of the contacts she'd made after leaving college, and had already been in touch with two very interested parties who liked the sample photos she'd sent them.

Her thoughts gravitated back to Jarrett. The idea of him using his sister's invitation to seize a chance to view the house at close quarters seriously bothered Sophia. She didn't know if that *had* been his motivation for a fact, but still she preferred the notion that it was her company he sought and *not* a closer acquaintance with her home. Warning herself not to forget even for a second that she'd sworn off relationships with men for good after enduring the living nightmare that had been her marriage, she determinedly buried the familiar feelings of failure and loneliness and reaffirmed her vow to put any further thoughts of Jarrett Gaskill aside.

Feeling somewhat calmer at this resolve, she carefully transported her still sleeping son inside the house. Settling him down on the threadbare old couch, she decided to let him doze for a little longer…at least until she'd prepared their dinner.

To please his sister, Jarrett did what she told him he was so naturally adept at and effortlessly mingled and chatted to her and her husband's friends at the little *soirée* she'd arranged—even though he secretly *hated* it. He did enough schmoozing at the corporate functions and meetings relating to his property business without replicating the behaviour in his supposed free time.

It was rare that he had a weekend off, and when he did he much preferred to be left to his own devices. He liked to take long walks in the countryside surrounding his house, listen to opera on his state-of-the-art music centre or catch up on the stack of films he had missed at the cinema because he'd inevitably been working. Yet agreeing to be sociable with his sister's friends and neighbours wasn't the *only* reason that he'd agreed to be present at her house this warm spring Saturday afternoon. All week Jarrett had hardly been able to think about anything but seeing Sophia Markham again. He couldn't forget the sight of her beautiful emerald eyes bathed in tears. It troubled him that she might be sad or lonely, yet if he was honest underneath his compassion he couldn't help wondering if there might be a way to persuade her to sell High Ridge to him. Painting her sitting room by herself didn't suggest that money was exactly plentiful, he mused. And if she agreed to entertain the idea of selling he would pay her a more than fair price.

His hopes lifting, Jarrett looked forward even more to seeing Sophia again. But the get-together had been underway for almost two hours and he was getting bored. There was only so much inconsequential chitchat he could bear, even for his sister, and there was still no sign of Sophia, although Beth assured him that she'd rung to say she was coming.

He was just debating whether to go up to the house and check to see if anything was amiss when the doorbell's familiar cheery melody chimed through the hallway. As luck would have it he was standing in the vicinity, endeavouring to listen attentively to his brother-in-law Paul's enthusiastic description of the new car he was going to buy. Privately he thought it was a bad choice, and he had just been thinking he would have a quiet word with Beth about it so she could nudge him in the direction of something better when the doorbell had rung. Without a flicker of guilt he moved down the hall to answer it. His body was already tightening warmly in anticipation of seeing High Ridge's lovely new owner again.

'Hi...I'm sorry if we're a little late.'

The statement came out in a breathless rush, and Sophia Markham's apologetic smile as he opened the door rendered him almost speechless because it was so bewitching.

Waiting patiently for his response, she drew Charlie protectively against her side. It wasn't hard to see that the child meant the sun, moon and stars to her.

Staring at her as she stood before him, in faded jeans, colourful knitted tank-top and long un-buttoned navy blue cardigan, he likened her appearance to a breath of longed-for fresh air that a prisoner might greedily gulp down when he'd been freed from solitary confinement. Today her pretty dark hair hadn't been left loose to flow down over her shoulders—instead she'd fashioned it into two very becoming braids. In contrast, the other women at the small party had seized the opportunity to show off their wardrobes and were dressed up to the nines. Personally, Jarrett thought such a brash display was unnecessary and over the top. He himself had dressed in a casual white shirt and black jeans faded almost to grey—his usual mode of attire when he wasn't at work—and he was very glad to see that Sophia had opted to do the same.

'Don't worry about being late... Beth will

kill me for saying it, but you've haven't exactly missed anything. It's good to see you.' After speaking at last, he grinned, then leaned down to squeeze Charlie's shoulder. 'It's good to see you too, Charlie. Why don't you both come inside?'

'Hello, there, I'm Paul Harvey—Beth's husband. How nice to meet you at last, Ms Markham.'

'And you, Mr Harvey.'

'Call me Paul.'

Sophia didn't invite the other man to call her by her first name in return, Jarrett noticed, silently approving. He had no earthly right to feel so possessive towards her, but for reasons he couldn't begin to explain he *did*.

'Let's go and meet everyone,' he suggested, gesturing for her and her son to precede him.

The conversations that littered the air as they walked in abruptly ceased as Jarrett escorted Sophia into the stylishly furnished living room. Even the softly playing jazz emanating from the music centre seemed to grow quieter. His sister Beth immediately peeled herself away from the trio of women she'd been deep in conversation with and presented herself to her new guest with an enthusiastic handshake, followed by the characteristic peck on the cheek with which she greeted all her friends.

'Hi, Sophia, I'm Beth Harvey—Jarrett's sister. I had no idea you'd be so pretty! I'm so glad you could come...your son too. Jarrett tells me that his name is Charlie?'

'That's right.'

Inside that perfectly decorated room, with its carefully chosen, strategically arranged amalgam of modern and antique furniture, surrounded by a bunch of curious strangers, Sophia looked ill at ease. Her coral lips were pursed together tightly as she listened to his sister gush, and Jarrett intuited that she'd rather be anywhere else but here. He was intrigued to know what had persuaded her to put in an appearance at all. Clearly she'd wrestled with the decision for some time—why else had she been so late in arriving? Something else struck him. He'd always regarded the sister who shared his own dramatic colouring of ebony hair and blue eyes as unquestionably pretty.

However, next to Sophia's finely drawn beautiful features and bewitching emerald eyes Beth seemed merely attractive.

Frowning, because he felt such an opinion somehow betrayed his loyalty to his sibling, he gently touched his palm to her back in the fitted red dress she was wearing, as if to signal filial support.

'Say hello, Charlie,' Sophia quietly instructed her son.

Bestowing upon Jarrett a gap-toothed grin, the charming small boy with his mop of luxuriant dark curls focused his gaze on him alone. 'Hello, Mr Gaskill. Can I see your sister's dog? Where is he?'

'You've met Dylan before, have you?' Beth dropped down so that she was level with Charlie.

The boy was initially wary, but when she reached for his hand and gently held it for a moment, smiling at him with her great blue eyes, he seemed to relax. 'Yes...we were down by the stream so that my mum could take some photographs for her work. That's when we saw Mr Gaskill and your dog.'

'Well, if you'd like to see him again he's out in the garden, sitting outside his kennel.'

'What's a kennel?'

'It's like a small house for a dog,' Jarrett told him with a teasing wink.

Charlie spun round to gaze up at his mother. 'Can I, Mummy? Can I go out to see Dylan?'

Such an innocent and natural request shouldn't put panic into Sophia's lovely green eyes, but disturbingly Jarrett registered that it did. She even laid a hand possessively on Charlie's shoulder as if to prevent him from leaving.

'Where is the garden?' she immediately quizzed Beth.

'Just out there through the patio doors... Don't worry, it's nowhere near big enough for him to get lost in.'

Biting down on her lip, Sophia was still undoubtedly hesitant. 'I'm sure that's true. There isn't a gate at the back he can get out of?'

'No, there isn't.'

'That's good. Our own garden is a bit like a forest, and I have to keep a close eye on Charlie when he goes out there to play. I suppose I've just got into the habit of making sure he's secure.' She coloured, as if regretting calling attention to her own hardly humble abode. 'It needs a lot of work doing to it, I'm afraid.' she murmured. 'The weeds have gone absolutely rampant in all this rain we've been having, but I'm getting the house into shape before I see to the garden.'

Rising to her full height once again, Beth reassuringly patted the other woman's arm. 'Well, compared to the gardens at High Ridge our garden is fairly modest, I promise you. Charlie can't get lost out there. And there are no ponds or anything like that to worry about either. Besides, he'll have Dylan to play with. Do you want to get his ball and throw it for him, Charlie?'

'Yes, please!' The lad didn't need much inducement.

'His ball is in a box just under the steps,' Beth told him.

As Sophia reluctantly released the light grip on

his shoulder, as if intuiting his mother's concern, Charlie turned to throw her a disarming grin. 'I'll be all right, Mummy—promise!' he said, and without further ado he flew out through the open patio doors onto the decking area, where two long tables were laden with platters of what remained of the delicious food Beth had prepared.

The repast still looked appetising in the watery spring sunshine, even though the hungry guests had helped themselves to a fair amount of it already.

Pounding down the wooden steps, fetching the dog's ball and racing out into the neatly mown garden, Charlie called loudly, 'Dylan! Dylan! Do you remember me? I'm Charlie. Come here, boy!'

'I'll introduce you to everyone in a moment—but first let me get you a drink, Sophia.'

Beth cleverly brought the other woman's attention back from her anxious perusal of her disappearing son. Paul had joined them just as Charlie had run out into the garden, and now Jarrett's sister turned to him with one of the dazzling persuasive smiles that her husband had always found so hard to resist.

'Darling? Would you be a love and get Sophia a nice glass of champagne?'

'No!'

The loud, vehement refusal sent a buzz of shock eddying round the other guests—Jarrett included…

CHAPTER THREE

SHE felt like a fool, blurting out her refusal as forcefully as she had. As soon as the impassioned exclamation had left her mouth Sophia had wanted the floor to open up and swallow her. It made her feel like the one jarring note in a symphony that had been harmonious until her arrival. Yet, blunt as her refusal had been, she had good reason to detest alcohol. Living with a violent alcoholic whose behaviour had been coloured by terrifying unpredictable rages was apt to make a woman deeply despise it—*fear* it as well.

'I'm sorry,' she murmured, reddening. 'I just meant to say that I'm teetotal. Do you have some lemonade or cola, perhaps, instead?'

'Sure. No problem.'

Paul Harvey shoved his hands into the pockets of his chinos and Sophia saw that his initially welcoming manner was now tinged with wariness. It made her bitterly regret deciding to attend the party. It was true she'd wrestled with the idea of staying away. *That was why she and Charlie had arrived so late.* As her host turned away to get the promised soft drink, his wife Beth issued her a sympathetic smile. Along with her guests, no doubt she was privately wondering at the reason why the newest member of the village should have reacted to the offer of champagne so violently.

Sophia prayed that the other woman wouldn't take it upon herself to quiz her at any point. The last thing she felt like doing was explaining herself to her perfect-looking hostess with her perfect-looking life, friends and husband. How could such a protected woman even *begin* to understand the pain, degradation and humiliation of the life Sophia had led with her husband? And all the reasons *why* she hated alcohol?

Silently warring with the strongest urge to just turn around and leave, she let her anxious gaze fall into Jarrett's. His strong brow was etched with the faintest frown, yet when his clear blue eyes met hers he somehow transmitted reassurance. She found herself latching onto it like a life raft.

Jarrett didn't yet know what Sophia's issues with alcohol were, but he was determined to find out. He'd genuinely hoped that this party would help her to make some friends, so that she and Charlie wouldn't feel like isolated strangers in the community for long, but already he sensed that her unconventional appearance—not bowing to the dictates of current fashion trends—and her forthright refusal of an alcoholic drink had put the other guests on their guard.

Unfortunately the insular nature of village life didn't exactly nurture a broader view in its inhabitants, he mused. He was thankful that he had seen enough of the world to know that it was the *differences* in people that made them interesting. But he also realised that his desire to help her integrate could turn out to be much more complicated than he'd envisaged. *He* had been the one to encourage her to come to this little get-together of his sister's and now, without being party to the reasons why, he saw for himself that what might be deemed an enjoyable experience by others might actually be *torture* for her. Observing her flushed cheeks and over-bright eyes, it wasn't hard to guess that what she'd really like to do was escape as soon as possible.

'Sophia?' He stepped towards the slim brunette, but not so close that he might overwhelm her. 'Why don't you and I go and join Charlie and Dylan in the garden? We'll get your drink on the way, and go sit on the veranda outside the summerhouse.'

Her relief was palpable. Right then, observing her shining green eyes and schoolgirl plaits, Jarrett thought her the very personification of beauty and innocence, and all his protective instincts surged to the fore, making his heart miss a disturbing beat. It was easy to forget about his desire to purchase High Ridge for himself when he was with her. Yet the thought still occurred that it might help persuade her to sell if he seriously started to woo her.

In the large, meticulously mown garden, with its uniformly neat borders of flowers and shrubs, Jarrett sat down next to Sophia on the varnished wooden bench outside the white-painted summerhouse. He silently observed her son throwing the ball to Dylan. The dog's dark eyes and wagging tail gave the impression he couldn't believe his luck that somebody wanted to play with him.

Folding her slim, elegant hands with their short unvarnished nails round her glass of lemonade, Sophia drew in a long breath, then softly released it. 'They look like they're having fun,' she commented, her glance cautiously alighting on Jarrett.

'Labradors and small boys were meant to be together,' he agreed, silently owning to feeling more content at this moment, in this lovely woman's company, than he could remember having felt in a long time. The revelation was an unexpected and tantalising gift that made the idea of wooing her even stronger.

Several guests had moved outside with their refreshments onto the patio, he noticed, and immediately the sight put him on his guard. Every now and then they glanced over at Jarrett and his companion, clearly speculating on their apparent closeness. He made a point of deliberately meeting their glances and staring right back.

'It's a shame that Beth and Paul haven't got kids that can play with Dylan,' he commented, seeking to divert Sophia from the realisation that his sister's guests were paying them an inordinate amount of attention.

'How long have your sister and her husband been married?'

'About ten years, I think.'

'Do they want to have children?'

'They've said many times that if it happens it happens...but in the meantime they'll concentrate on their careers and just enjoy each other's company.'

'Are they happy?'

Pausing, Jarrett gave the question proper consideration. He had straight away registered the apprehension, hope and even *envy* in the arresting emerald eyes that studied him so fervently, and he guessed the answer was important to her. 'I think so.' He shrugged, smiling, then added, 'Although anyone can present an image of happiness, contentment and togetherness, can't they? In truth, only the individuals concerned know if they're happy or not.'

'I agree. Unfortunately if they seem happier than you, then you can feel a bit of a failure.'

Intrigued, Jarrett leaned forward a little.

'Have you ever asked yourself why happiness seems to come so easily to some and not to others?' she pondered. 'Do you think it's got anything to do with *deserving* it?'

'No. I don't think it's got anything to do with deserving it,' he replied. 'There are too many examples in the world to disprove that. Why? Has someone told you that it has?'

'No. Maybe I just feel too guilty about the wrong turns I've made.'

'It sounds to me as if you're much too hard on yourself. Maybe if you could just dump all the guilt that weighs you down and try to be more optimistic things might get a little easier for you, Sophia? I know you can't control everything that happens in life, but I must confess I'm a strong believer in creating your own luck…being captain of your own ship.'

'Oh.'

'Do you have other views on the matter?'

Working her even white teeth against her plump lower lip, Sophia lightly shook her head. 'I do— but I think they might be somewhat prejudiced. I started out being very optimistic about life…convinced that I knew which road to take to make me happy. But although I remained optimistic and hopeful I made some very poor decisions that made me anything *but*. Let's just leave it at that, shall we?'

'We all make poor decisions and mistakes from time to time. It comes with the territory of being human. It doesn't mean that you won't ever make a good decision again and achieve some level of satisfaction and happiness.'

'I'm sure you're right.'

'Going back to your original question about my sister and her husband—what's your impression? Do *you* think that they're happy?'

'Well, I've only just met them, but if this extremely tidy garden is any indication I get the impression that they live a very ordered and potentially happy life together.'

'Beth and Paul are both very practical people. I'd never call them dreamers, if that's what you're getting at.'

Hunching forward to rest his elbows on his knees, he examined the neat borders with new eyes, almost guiltily recalling Beth's account of her several visits to a local garden centre for advice on creating the perfect lawn. The very concept had bemused him.

'And, yes, they don't appear to leave very much to chance,' he agreed cautiously.

'Dreamers or not, life has a way of subverting even the most carefully laid plans.'

Sophia gazed off into the distance, as if preoccupied by some disturbing recollection that still haunted her. Turning to observe her, Jarrett felt his insides submerged in a wave of sympathy.

A second later Charlie called out to her to watch him throw the ball, and her lovely face broke into an unguarded smile, the disturbing memory temporarily banished. 'That's wonderful, darling!'

'You should learn to play cricket, Charlie,' Jarrett called out. 'You're a natural bowler.'

'Will you teach me, Mr Gaskill?'

'I'd be delighted to…but only if you call me Jarrett.'

The small boy gifted him with a self-conscious grin. 'Okay!'

'That's settled, then.'

'You shouldn't promise him things that you don't have the time or the intention to follow through on,' Sophia scolded him, her cheeks flushing pink. 'He has a memory like an elephant. He forgets nothing…even the things I wish he *would*.'

It was the last part of her statement that perturbed Jarrett the most. Now wasn't the time, but very soon he fully intended to ask her exactly what she meant by it. He also wanted to ask why she'd commented that she wasn't sorry she was a widow. That discussion they'd just had about happiness was already taking on a significance that he wanted to explore.

Depositing his glass of wine on the small wrought-iron table in front of them, he suddenly pushed to his feet. 'What makes you think I wouldn't keep my promise?' he asked, irked that she would doubt him.

'He's been let down by people breaking their promises to him before, and I don't want him building up hopes only to have them dashed again.'

'Not everyone breaks their promises. Maybe you need to learn to trust a little bit more?'

'Trust *you*, you mean? I barely know you.'

'That can be remedied.'

She lifted a slim, nonchalant shoulder to indicate her ambivalence, but Jarrett saw her lips duel unsuccessfully with her natural inclination to smile. Satisfied at the sight, he grinned, then hurried down the veranda steps, calling out to the boy on the lawn at the same time, 'Throw me that ball, Charlie, and we'll see how good you are at catching!'

Returning to the kitchen a while later to replenish their drinks, he found his sister standing at the sink, staring out of the window into the garden as she expertly rinsed some used glasses.

'I've been watching you playing with Charlie. You looked like you were really enjoying yourself,' she remarked.

'Why so surprised? I *do* have the ability to enjoy myself, you know.'

'It's just that you looked quite bored until Sophia arrived…then you lit up.' Beth turned to give him an affectionate smile. 'I'm pleased that you seem to enjoy their company so much.'

'I don't deny it. She intrigues me, and Charlie is a great little boy.'

Walking forward to rinse the empty glasses he'd brought with him, Jarrett wasn't surprised when Beth took them from him and set them down on the drainer.

'You don't have to wash the glasses. Just leave

them and get some fresh ones.' Frowning, she dried her hands on a teatowel, then patted down her hair. 'I've just been standing here thinking about Sophia. She strikes me as quite a troubled person. I wonder what's behind that sad look in her eyes. She seems very protective of her son.'

'And that's a crime, is it?'

'Don't be silly. Of course it isn't. But everybody who heard her hesitate about letting him play out in the garden thought it was a little over the top.'

'Ah.' Folding his arms across his chest, Jarrett endeavoured not to let irritation get the better of him. 'So it's a case of the majority rules, is it?'

'It's only natural that people speculate. Think about it. Sophia appears out of nowhere and moves into the most coveted house in the district when the place wasn't even up for sale. Is there some family connection? If so, why not let it be known? It arouses suspicion when people are so secretive. My guess is that there was some kind of tragedy in her life before she came here. Something to do with Charlie's father, perhaps.'

Jarrett was so taken aback by this observation

that for a moment words deserted him. Then he sighed, disturbed because Beth was probably right. *What if, for instance, Sophia's husband had done the unthinkable and taken his own life?* Maybe he'd suffered from depression and that was why she'd alluded to the fact that the marriage had been unhappy?

'If that turns out to be the case then all anyone can do is offer sympathy and kindness and not judge her. Don't you agree?' he said.

Lifting her shoulders in a somewhat chastened shrug, his sister visibly softened her expression. 'You're right.' But, clearly unable to put the matter to bed entirely, she added, 'Has she said anything to you?'

'No, she hasn't. It's not likely that she'd confide in *me* about anything, is it? Since we've only just met?' Quirking an eyebrow, Jarrett made his way across to the counter that was laden with cartons of juice and bottles of wine. 'I'd better get our drinks and get back to her.'

'It's not just because she owns High Ridge that you find yourself attracted to her, is it?'

'What?' He spun round, his heart drumming a dizzying tattoo inside his chest.

'Don't be mad at me for asking. It's just that I know you've always loved the place. Perhaps you're hoping that if you become friends she'll consider selling it to you?'

'I think we'd better end this conversation right here.'

He'd been seriously intent on wooing Sophia, but Beth's comments made him fear that she was viewing him solely as the hard-headed landowner he was reputed to be. A man who wouldn't hesitate to be mercenary if it suited him, rather than the amiable brother she loved. Her good opinion mattered to him. The bright afternoon was suddenly soured.

Irked, Jarrett left her in the kitchen, shouldering past the guests outside on the patio and deliberately ignoring any attempts to engage him in conversation. Surprised glances followed him into the garden as he made a beeline across the grass to the pretty woman still sitting on the bench outside the veranda.

Catching hold of her hand, he pulled her to her feet. 'I think it's time that we left.'

'Why? What's wrong?'

Instantly regretting being the instigator of what looked like fear in her eyes, Jarrett abruptly let go of Sophia's hand and took a deep breath to compose himself. 'It's my fault. I should never have persuaded you that it was a good idea to come here today. How do you feel about my taking you and Charlie to the seaside instead? There's still plenty of daylight left. If you want to stop off at home to collect your camera so that you can take some pictures you can do that. We'll drive down in my car.'

Regarding the earnest expression on his handsome face, and trying hard to ignore the bolt of electricity that had shot through her insides when he'd grabbed her hand, Sophia couldn't deny that Jarrett's impromptu suggestion was appealing. But, even so, the memory of past wrong decisions aroused her caution.

'Do you really think I should risk going with

you anywhere when I hardly even know you?'
she asked.

He held her gaze with a long and steady stare.
'You're getting to know me…you know my name
and who I am. You also know who my sister is
and where she lives, and there are plenty of other
people here who could testify to seeing us leave
together. Isn't that enough to reassure you that
I'm no sinister stranger with unsavoury motives?'

Sophia was indeed reassured. She smiled.
'Okay, I'll go to the seaside with you…Charlie
will be ecstatic at the idea. But first I want you
to tell me what's made you suddenly decide we
should leave.'

Dropping his hands to his lean jean-clad hips,
Jarrett glanced down at the ground, as if to glean
inspiration as to how best to answer, then raised
his head and scowled. 'Excluding yourself and
Charlie, let's just say the company isn't as charming as I thought it would be.'

Now it was Sophia's turn to be dismayed.
Someone must have said something unflattering about her. But even though she was curi-

ous to know what had been said, she knew it was a pointless and self-destructive exercise to find out. After what she and Charlie had been through what could it possibly matter what anyone thought of her? *Especially* people she didn't know and who didn't know her?

'Let's get out of here.' Obviously impatient to be gone, Jarrett glanced over at Charlie, who was still throwing the ball for an excitable Dylan to fetch.

Sophia touched his sleeve to get his attention. 'If someone's running me down I'm quite capable of standing up for myself, you know. You don't need to act as my protector.'

'No one's running you down. People are just curious about you, and I don't want you to feel inhibited by what you imagine they think of you.' Shaking his head, he hunted her with his azure gaze so that there was nowhere for her to hide. 'I've sensed since we met that something bad happened before you came here…something you want to escape from. You told me that you're a widow but that you aren't sorry about the fact.

I'm not asking you to reveal the details about what happened right now, but all I'll say is that if you've been hurt by someone I don't intend for you to be hurt again by people's narrow-minded suspicions.'

'I see.'

Whilst she'd already told him that she didn't need him to act as her protector, Sophia couldn't deny the wave of warmth that his compassionate defence stirred inside her. It was an exhilarating feeling, and she wondered what she had done to deserve it. Having dealt with her problems single-handedly for so long, it was irresistibly comforting to have someone exhibit compassion towards her.

Just when Jarrett seemed about to make another plea for them to leave, she lifted a slender brow, smiled, and asked lightly, 'Does our little trip to the seaside include food? It's just that you're dragging us away from that incredible-looking feast up there on the patio and I'm feeling rather hungry.'

'I'll treat you both to a five course meal at a swanky restaurant, if that's any inducement?'

'You don't need to go that far. Charlie and I are extremely partial to a bit of fish and chips at the seaside.'

With a cheeky grin that squeezed Jarrett's heart, Sophia swept past him to inform her son about the sudden change of plans.

Not only had Sophia collected her camera by the time Jarrett had followed her and Charlie home in his Range Rover, but she'd also picked up her son's swim-trunks, towel, and a bucket and spade.

When they got to the beach she made a foray into the frigid sea in her rolled-up jeans and shirt—with a shrieking Charlie splashing about beside her—whilst Jarrett stood barefoot in the sand calmly watching them, declaring that they must be mad to even *think* of immersing themselves in such freezing cold water. Though she didn't turn round to check, Sophia sensed his eyes on her as though they were twin suns burning into her skin. Just the thought of him observing her was enough to make her temperature rise, despite the cold of the sea.

To distract herself from the realisation, she dipped her hands into the water, spun round and aimed what she'd collected at Jarrett. The water hit him straight in the face.

'I can't believe you just did that.' He rubbed at his dripping eyelids and scowled.

Laughing out loud at his shocked expression, Sophia couldn't prepare herself for his reaction. Never mind that he was going to get soaked, Jarrett raced up beside her, grabbed her by the waist and lifted her high into his arms.

Charlie could scarcely contain his delight. 'What are you going to do with my mummy, Mr Jarrett?' he squealed.

'All's fair in love and war, Charlie.' Directing the comment at Sophia, Jarrett gave her an unashamedly roguish grin.

Her heart thumped in alarm when she realised that he was probably going to dump her fully clothed into the sea, so she fastened her arms round his neck and made her expression as fierce as she was able. 'Don't you *dare*! If you do I'll take you with me, I swear!'

'That's a puny threat. I'm twice your size. You're hardly strong enough to take me down with you.'

'Try me!' Sophia warned.

But as her furious gaze locked with his the volatile tenor of the situation changed completely to something far more exciting and disturbing to her peace of mind. His nearness, along with the sexily musky aroma of his cologne, made her feel dangerously weak. Not just weak but *aroused*... Straight away she saw by Jarrett's darkened pupils that she was having the same effect on him.

'Maybe I'll save the dunking for another day,' he commented huskily, then abruptly returned her to her feet and the freezing water that lapped the shore.

Murmuring, 'In your dreams...' to hide her embarrassment, Sophia directed her full attention back to her son. 'Come on, Charlie, let's run towards the waves and run back again before they reach us!'

By the time she and Charlie ran back onto the shore, a few minutes later, Jarrett was waiting with the generous sized bathtowel she'd brought from home. Catching her eye, he smiled as if to reassure her he held no grudges about her splashing him with ice-cold seawater. Then he unhesitatingly wrapped the towel around Charlie, as if genuinely concerned that he get warm and dry again as quickly as possible.

Sophia was certain that anyone observing them would assume that he was the boy's father. Their colouring—apart from the eyes, of course—was practically identical. The notion gave her the strangest most unsettling pang. Jarrett was bigger, leaner and more muscular in build than her husband Tom had been…taller too. It wasn't likely that Charlie would reach a similar height. Yet he would undoubtedly be handsome when he was grown.

Ruffling her son's damp corkscrew curls, Jarrett stood aside so that Sophia could finish off the drying and help him get dressed. With his T-shirt and shorts on again, Charlie was eager to collect some seashells, so he skipped a little bit further on down the beach with his red bucket and spade, his mother's clear instruction to not wander out of her sight ringing in his ears. Deliberately avoiding glancing directly at Jarrett, because his commanding masculine presence was making her feel painfully self-conscious, she lifted her long, drenched plaits off the back of her neck, arranged the towel round her shoulders and stooped to pick up the straw bag with the spare set of clothing that she'd left lying on the sand next to her sandals. Her jeans and shirt were plastered icily to her skin where Charlie had splashed her.

'I'm going over by those rocks to change,' she told Jarrett, finally meeting his arresting cobalt gaze. 'Would you keep an eye on Charlie for me?'

'No problem. I'll go and join him to help collect seashells.'

Even though they'd spent a thoroughly enjoyable afternoon together on the beach, and at the small seaside restaurant where they'd had fish and chips, Jarrett honestly hadn't expected Sophia to invite him in when they reached High Ridge. But fate was on his side. Charlie had fallen asleep in his car seat.

Sophia got out of the car, peered in at him, then glanced round at Jarrett with an almost apologetic shrug. 'Would you mind carrying him into the house for me? I'll grab our things and open the door.'

On entering the hallway, he saw the ceiling with its old-fashioned cornices was far loftier than he'd anticipated, but the overall impression Jarrett got was that the place was as dark and dingy as Miss Havisham's decaying manor in *Great Expectations*. The remaining evening light that did manage to stream in through the front door's decorated windowpanes was nowhere near illuminating enough to make the place remotely welcoming. Underfoot was an equally dingy, well-trodden maroon carpet that in his view ought to be replaced, or at least given a professional clean.

As he followed Sophia into the house, carefully

transporting her still-sleeping little boy in his arms, he couldn't help reflecting that he'd love to help restore the place to its former beauty. But even as the thought stole into his mind Jarrett's sight was helplessly waylaid by the graceful sway of the lithe yet shapely hips of the pretty woman in front of him. Her long slim legs along with the peach-like derrière snugly enclosed in a pair of almost shabby blue jeans suspended any further reflections bar the realisation that he *wanted* her. From the moment he'd seen her lissome shapely figure outlined by the clinging jeans and shirt at the beach, and briefly lifted her into his arms, he'd ached with every fibre of his being to be intimate with her—and soon.

'You can put him down on the couch,' his lovely companion instructed him, her porcelain cheeks flushing a little as her emerald eyes warily met his.

He willingly complied—but not before thinking how much he'd love to free her beautiful chestnut hair from the plaits she'd worn all day, knowing that it would ripple down her back like a pre-Raphaelite beauty's. Jarrett had a powerful compulsion to comb out the long silken skeins with his fingers, then gently smooth them back so that he could more closely examine the sublime contours of her lovely face.

'I can carry him up to bed if you'd prefer?'

Sophia declined the offer. 'He'll be fine right here on the couch. We don't use the bedrooms upstairs. There's a lot of work to be done to make them anywhere near habitable, I'm afraid. Charlie and I sleep in what was once the parlour. I've cleaned it up a bit, got rid of the dust and cobwebs—that sort of thing. I've put up some new curtains and arranged our beds in there. There's even a fireplace that we can use in the winter if need be. The house doesn't have the luxury of central heating, and I'm sure the temperatures will be bitter by then.'

After gently pulling the colourful crocheted blanket that lay folded at the end of the antique sofa over Charlie's sleeping form, Jarrett straightened to give her his undivided attention. 'I don't mean this unkindly, but did you even know what you were doing when you bought a place like this?'

Sophia dropped the straw bag she'd taken to the seaside onto a nearby Edwardian chair and folded her arms. Then she lifted her chin in a gesture that clearly illustrated her defensiveness. 'I didn't buy it. Do I look like the kind of person who could afford to buy a house like this?'

He shrugged. 'What *does* a person who can afford to buy an expensive period property look like? If you didn't buy it, then how did you come to be here?' Sensing this wasn't the kind of information she readily wanted to share, he almost held his breath as he silently willed her not to keep it a secret.

Absently freeing the two covered red bands that secured her plaits, she started to loosen her hair. *Jarrett's mouth turned helplessly dry as he watched her comb her slender fingers through it.* Just as he'd imagined, the luxurious fall of rippling dark strands might have come straight out of a pre-Raphaelite painting.

'My aunt left it to me.'

'Mary Wingham was your aunt?'

'My great-aunt.'

Taken aback for a moment, he rubbed a hand round his jaw. 'Did you visit her much when she was alive?'

She looked downcast. 'No. I didn't. The last time I was here was when I was about twelve years old.'

'Yet she bequeathed you this house?'

'Yes.'

'She must have been very fond of you.'

'Hmm.' The soft green eyes glimmered wryly. 'My dad always told me she didn't exactly like our family...although I think she secretly had a bit of a soft spot for him. Anyway, the last time I personally set eyes on her was at his funeral, and I remember her looking pretty upset. But I still don't know why she chose to leave the place to me. Of course I'm very grateful that she did.'

'But—'

'I'm tired, and I really think I've answered enough questions for one day.'

Even though he yearned to hear more, the expression on Sophia's face was determined enough to make Jarrett conclude he shouldn't push his luck—and neither should he forget that for a woman who had an obvious tendency to be reclusive she had at least let her guard down enough to allow him to spend time with her and her son.

CHAPTER FOUR

TELLING herself it would be rude not to offer Jarrett a cup of tea when he'd so thoughtfully taken her and Charlie to the beach for the afternoon, Sophia fought down her wariness at his curiosity about her and led the way into the lofty-ceilinged kitchen. With its dulled terracotta tiled floor and tall curtainless windows overlooking the currently wild and untended back garden, it was hardly inviting.

Seeing the daylight was fading fast, she flicked on the light switch. But the pool of dreary yellow light emanating weakly from the single bulb hovering above the scrubbed pine table in its nondescript cream shade hardly helped matters. It was hard for her not to feel painfully embarrassed that the room wasn't more hospitable.

'How do you take your tea?' she asked her

guest, almost flinching as his penetrating gaze interestedly examined his surroundings. There was no way they'd make a favourable comparison with his sister's ultra-modern fitted kitchen, she thought. Not unless his preference was for genteel old buildings in urgent need of a major makeover.

'I like it strong, thanks…no sugar. What an incredible kitchen—great for a large family. Beautiful too.'

'It certainly could be. Of course I plan to renovate it, along with the rest of the house, but I can't afford to do it all straight away. It's going to take an awful lot of money and time to do it justice. It's clear that my aunt got rather frail towards the end of her life and couldn't take care of the place like she used to. When I visited here as a child it always seemed so grand. It was like a palace, and the garden was a fairy princess's magical kingdom.'

One corner of Jarrett's lips hitched up into his cheek. 'That's a nice memory. You know, Sophia, some things are worth waiting for. With a house like this it makes good sense to take your time mulling over what you'd like to do room by room. Just do what you can when you can. One step at a time, would be my advice.'

'Why don't you sit down?' Making a cursory nod towards one of the straight-backed chairs round the table, Sophia was a little taken aback by Jarrett's measured comments, but she also felt reassured that he sympathised and understood.

'Sophia?'

'Yes?' Glancing round as she stood at the deep ceramic butler sink, filling the copper kettle at the single tap, she was slightly unnerved by the intensity of his gaze. He was standing behind the chair rather than sitting down, and his big hands curled round the dark wooden back as though he were indelibly stamping his presence on everything he touched…disturbingly on her *senses* too…whether she liked it or not.

'You seem a little on edge,' he observed. 'Why don't you try and relax?'

'I'm afraid it's become rather a habit…*not* being able to relax, I mean.'

'Because of what happened to you before you came here?'

The sonorous chiming of the grandfather clock in the hallway just then drowned out any other sound. It also gave Sophia some precious moments to collect her thoughts. 'What do you mean?'

'I think you know what I mean... But I'll ask you plainly so that there's no confusion.'

Turning off the tap, she lifted the kettle with a less than steady hand, then set it down on the wooden draining board. She turned to face him. 'Go on, then.'

'You told me that you were a widow. But the comment you made straight afterwards about not being sorry about it definitely suggested your marriage wasn't a happy one. Was that the reason you came to the village and moved into your aunt's house rather than selling it?'

'You think I was running away from a bad marriage?'

'I'm not suggesting that wouldn't have been the right thing to do if you were dreadfully unhappy.'

'Look, I want you to know that I'm not comfortable with you so freely expressing your opinions about my life, and nor am I happy about you asking all these questions. Perhaps you should respect my right to privacy a little more?'

Jarrett sucked in a breath through his teeth. 'Maybe if you were just someone I ran into now and again—someone who meant nothing to me—then I most definitely *would*. But I'm sure you've guessed by now that I've become quite intrigued by you.'

His statement might have quickened Sophia's heart if she'd been in a good place mentally and emotionally, but she knew she was far from feeling good enough about herself to accept it even for a second. The sensation of the cold ceramic sink pressing into her back added to her sense of feeling utterly chilled right then…desolate at the idea that life might never be good again, no matter how hard she prayed it would be. Now that her wonder and gratitude at her eleventh-hour reprieve of being gifted this beautiful house had started to fade a little, a sense of battle fatigue after what she'd endured had begun to seep into her bones.

'Well, you're wasting your time being intrigued,' she snapped, knowing that she was only being curt because she feared him getting too close and pursuing the idea of a relationship. 'I have nothing to offer you, Jarrett. I mean it. I really don't…particularly friendship. I'm in no position to be a friend to anybody—*even* myself. If you knew my unerring ability to take wrong turns and make disastrous decisions, trust me, you'd avoid me like the plague. You'd be much better off directing your interest towards the kind of women that were at your sister's party today… women who are completely at ease with making social small talk, who are undemanding and uncomplicated and no doubt come from the kind of comfortable world where what everything looks like is far more important than being remotely real. That way at least you'd know *exactly* what you'd be getting.'

Glowering, Jarrett angrily pushed away from the chair, and the ear-splitting sound of wood scraping against the red stone flags made Sophia gasp. Breathing hard, he planted himself directly in front of her. One glance up into his hot and fierce blue eyes made her head feel as if it was spinning. Above the pounding of her heart she could hardly hear her own panicked thoughts.

'I might be materially comfortable, but I'm not superficial. Where did you get that unflattering impression from? Do you think you're the only person who's ever made a mistake or a disastrous decision? And, for your information, I neither want nor desire *any* of the women you've just described. They might be my sister's friends but they're not mine. And the fact that you've immediately intuited what they're all about must surely tell you *why* I wouldn't be interested in them.'

Despite her heart hammering at his nearness, and also because for one dreadful moment his action had brought back a sickening memory of Tom, furiously lashing out at her because she'd displeased him in some way, Sophia schooled herself to stay calm. The man standing in front of her *wasn't* Tom. And, even though she'd obviously hit a raw nerve by describing the world of his sister's friends as 'superficial', she somehow knew that Jarrett wasn't the kind of man who would use his superior strength to intimidate or wound a woman.

The breath she exhaled was undoubtedly relieved—but then another disturbing thought struck. 'Perhaps you're not interested in them because you're already involved with someone?'

'If you were interested in my relationship status then why didn't you ask me about it before? Do you think I'd offer to take you and Charlie to the seaside if I was involved with someone else?' As he crossed his arms over his chest, Jarrett's scowl turned into a perturbed frown.

Sophia heard what he said, but just then her attention was helplessly captured by the way the clearly defined muscles in his upper arms bunched and flexed beneath the loose-fitting material of his cotton shirt. The sight made her feel hot and bothered in a way that she hadn't experienced since she was eighteen...*before* Tom Abingdon had crushed all her innocent hopes and dreams of a happy, loving marriage deep into the dirt with his proclivity for cruelty and licentiousness.

'I'm sorry. Clearly my social skills aren't what they once were. I didn't mean to offend you.' Turning away in a bid to hide her heated reaction to him, she gasped when Jarrett fastened his hand lightly round her forearm.

'You haven't offended me.' His voice rolled over her senses like a warm sea of honey. Along with his touch, and the simmering heat in his gaze that he didn't trouble to disguise, it completely electrified her.

'Just so that you know, there's only one woman I'm interested in, Sophia, and that's *you*.'

'I already told you that I can't offer you anything. Weren't you listening?'

'I heard what you said. But I'm not a man who gives up easily when I sense something or *someone* might potentially be important to me.'

His riveting gaze made her feel as if she was diving into a molten blue lake. When he lifted his hand from her arm, Sophia knew the sensuous tingling imprint that he left on her skin would not easily vanish when he had gone. Apart from being immensely pleasurable, the thought of what it might mean…where it could lead should she succumb to his touch more fully…made her quake inside…

Putting a lit match to the tinder she'd arranged between the split ash logs in the once grand fireplace, it was with a real sense of satisfaction that Sophia watched the dry wooden limbs and scrunched-up newspaper catch fire. Her father had always loved a real fire in winter, or when the weather was sufficiently cold to warrant one, and they unfailingly reminded Sophia of home and of *him. Sometimes it was too much to bear to remember he was gone and that he'd left the world believing that his only daughter was in safe hands with her new husband.* But she'd often counted her blessings that he *hadn't* lived to see the misery Tom had inflicted on her, because it would have broken his heart. He would also have been furious that any man would treat her with anything but the utmost respect, and would have fought tooth and nail to extricate her from a marriage that in truth had been *doomed* even before the ceremony.

What she would give now to have had the common sense to see it for herself. Yet her union with her husband had not been a total disaster, because it had given her Charlie…the little boy who had helped Sophia cling to hope even when times had been unremittingly dark and frightening… The depth of love she felt for her son went way beyond any love she could ever imagine. She glanced over at him now, to check that he was still sleeping. Satisfied that he was, she allowed herself a pleased smile, then returned her gaze to the fire.

Flashes of blue flame were licking hotly round the fragrant logs, denoting the fire had taken firm hold, and she rose to her feet from her kneeling position in front of it, dusted her hands over her jeans and returned to the worn maroon armchair opposite her guest. Charlie continued to slumber blissfully in his curled-up position on the couch, his plump cheeks rosy as the sweetest red apple even though the warmth of the fire had not yet permeated the room. Sophia moved her glance to Jarrett. The long muscular legs in faded black denim were stretched out in a relaxed pose as he sipped at the mug of tea she'd made him, and she couldn't help admiring his apparent ability to be so at ease.

'Great idea of yours to light a fire,' he remarked, and his sinfully velvet-rich tones elicited an outbreak of goosebumps up and down her skin.

'It's cold enough for one,' she said and smiled. "Cast not a clout 'til May is out" my grandmother used to say—and it's true. Funny how the old sayings are such a comfort…even when you're little and don't understand them.'

'I know what you mean. Was the grandmother you mentioned your father's mother or your mother's?'

Making herself as comfortable as she could manage in the hard-backed armchair—not easy when the seat cushion beneath her was worn flat as a pancake from use and old-age—Sophia took a careful sip of her hot sweet tea, then lowered the mug to rest it against her denim-covered thigh. 'She was my dad's mum. My mother was an orphan. I didn't know any of her family. And, before you quiz me about that, don't you think it's time you told me a little bit about yourself?'

'Fair enough.' He leant forward a little, glinting blue eyes watching her with the same deceptively languid curiosity of a cat. 'What do you want to know?'

'Have you always lived round here?'

'No. I moved to the area about ten years ago, when my sister got married and set up home in the village. Before that I lived in lots of different places...mainly abroad.'

'I take it that you and Beth are close, then?'

Despite being irked that Beth had suspected him of trying to get close to Sophia in order to persuade her to sell him High Ridge, and hadn't entertained the idea that he genuinely liked her, Jarrett couldn't deny that they were indeed close.

'We lost our parents when we were in our teens. That kind of tragedy helps to forge a close-knit bond with a sibling. Beth is a couple of years older than me, and I suppose she took it upon herself to be my guardian. Unfortunately—even though I'm thirty-six and have been independent for a hell of a long time—she occasionally still likes to assume the role. Needless to say I hardly welcome it.'

'So you came back from your travels to be near her?'

'Perhaps.' Feeling uncomfortable at admitting as much, Jarrett was wary of Sophia judging him and making the assumption that he wasn't psychologically strong enough to get on with his life without Beth being close by. 'I think most people are always looking for a point of reference—a sense of belonging somewhere where they're unconditionally accepted and known…don't you?'

'You mean like home?'

His companion's voice softened audibly and her small, perfect hands curved round the cheerful yellow mug of tea as if to try and contain her feelings. 'Yes,' he answered, intuiting that her mind had wandered back into the past…perhaps back to the series of events that had led her to come to High Ridge and into a whole new mode of existence where she had to raise her son on her own.

The pretty green eyes that still glanced cautiously at him from beneath dark brown lashes were full of painful shadows, Jarrett saw. In that instant the compulsion to offer comfort was so strong that he scarcely knew what to do with it. But the last thing he wanted was to scare or overwhelm her. In the end he simply put down his mug of tea and bided his time until she started talking again.

'I'd like to make a home here too,' she confided at last, her tone wistful, 'for me and Charlie. But the truth is I don't know if I'll be able to. Not in this house anyway.'

'Why?'

'Look at the size of this place...the responsibility is overwhelming. You've only glimpsed how much work needs doing—and that's just the gardens and the downstairs. Upstairs there are eight rooms...*eight*! Thanks to my great-aunt Mary I own the house outright, but that doesn't mean I can afford to keep it.'

'You don't earn enough from your photography to maintain it and pay the bills?'

'You must be joking! I'm only starting to build my career after a long period of not being able to pursue it. I've managed to secure a couple of potentially lucrative commissions, thanks to some old contacts, but nowhere near enough work to be able to relax and not worry.'

Jarrett frowned. 'Didn't your late husband leave any provision for you and Charlie? At the very least he must have had life insurance?'

Sophia reddened and lowered her gaze. 'The answer is no to both those questions.' When she glanced up again, her expression easily revealed that memories of her husband still had the power to cause her tremendous pain. 'The only person he ever provided for was himself.'

'I see. I'm sorry.'

'The truth is, as much as I love the idea of spending the rest of my days living in this beautiful old house, maybe I should be a bit more realistic. Maybe what I need to do is just sell it and buy something a lot smaller and more manageable for Charlie and me.'

Jarrett could hardly believe what he was hearing. But even as his heart leapt at the possibility of making an offer to Sophia to buy High Ridge from her—the house that he'd long dreamt of owning—in all conscience he found he suddenly *couldn't*. It was already clear as crystal to him that she was looking for a safe haven from her painful past, and right now he intuited that this historic old house was *it*. She'd had family here... blood ties. That sense of an ancestral link, of familial continuity, more importantly of *belonging*, must be important to her and Charlie right now, given their situation.

Wasn't that why Jarrett himself had made his permanent home here? Just so that he could be near his sister? Because at the end of the day there was no one else who cared if he lived or died. Despite their sometimes vociferous differences of opinion, and her perhaps not-so-flattering speculation on his intentions earlier today, he firmly believed that family was important.

If his competitors ever learned that he hadn't leapt at the chance to secure High Ridge Hall, he didn't doubt they would seriously think that he'd lost that renowned single-minded steely edge that had helped make him one of the wealthiest landowners in the county. But right then Jarrett didn't care. For maybe the first time in his life he was genuinely considering someone else's well-being above his own. The truth was that Sophia Markham had *disarmed* him. The defences that he'd kept stoically intact for so long were swiftly and devastatingly crumbling every time he saw her...

'Jarrett? Did you hear what I said?'

'Hmm?' Distracted because his feelings had stolen a march on him, he stood up and crossed to the now blazing fire. 'If you want to make a home here for you and Charlie, then in my opinion I don't think you should give up on the idea of keeping the house simply because of finances. In the meantime I could make you a loan, if that would help? Then you wouldn't be reliant on getting more photographic commissions straight away. You could take your time sourcing more work. You could also pay for some of the essential repairs and renovation to be done on the house.'

Turning back to survey his companion, he didn't expect to find her expression so crestfallen. The glitter in her beautiful eyes immediately alerted him to the fact that she was crying. Jarrett's mouth dried in alarm.

'What on earth's the matter?'

'Even presuming that you can afford to make such a substantial loan, why would you do that for me?'

'Because I want to.' He shrugged, knowing there was no point in pretending otherwise. 'I want to help you in any way I can. Trust me...I can more than afford it.'

'You barely even know me.'

'You keep saying that. But I've got great hopes that you *will* let me get to know you better, Sophia.' Wondering how on earth he managed to contain the inflammatory urge that scorched through his blood right then, to haul her to her feet and kiss her, to taste the sweetly seductive strawberry lips that had unwittingly been taunting him all day, every time he so much as glanced at her, Jarrett exhaled a frustrated sigh. 'Then you won't be able to use the fact that we don't know each other well enough as an excuse.'

'No, Jarrett.' Firmly wiping away all trace of tears with the heel of her hand, Sophia rose to her feet and approached the mantelpiece. Leaving her mug of tea on the white marble shelf, she crossed her arms over her navy wool cardigan and turned to face him. 'I absolutely won't accept a loan from you. I either find my own way to finance this place or I *don't.*'

'It's admirable that you're so determined…but if you love this house as much as I'm guessing you do then it makes sense to accept some help when it's offered, doesn't it?'

The emerald eyes flashed. 'Can't you *see*? Can't you *tell* that I find the idea of being beholden to anyone for mine and Charlie's welfare abhorrent?'

Jarrett could indeed see that, and whilst he understood her very human need to remain independent—and honestly admired it—he guessed things weren't as simple or straightforward as that. More than once he'd witnessed fear in her eyes…*dread* even. It made him determined to discover why. He'd already gleaned that her husband hadn't been the best example of masculinity on earth, but was there more to it than that?

'Putting that topic aside for a minute, what about my getting to know you better?' He forced himself to ask the question, even though he feared her response wouldn't be the one he wanted. It had already dented his confidence that she'd refused his offer of a loan.

'You mean as a friend?'

'That would be a start, I suppose.' The wry quirk of his lips along with his slightly uneasy tone revealed that he hoped for much more than friendship…*so* much more.

Sophia's mesmerising emerald glance was

absolutely steady. 'If I had met you years ago, Jarrett…before I met my husband Tom…perhaps we would have been a good match. Who knows? You seem to have a lot of the qualities and attributes I used to hope to find in a man. But my experience of being in a relationship has been irredeemably damaged by Charlie's father. I don't have the hope or the innocence I once had to trust in another relationship or believe that it could work. Nor do I want you to think that there's the slightest chance that I'll change my mind, because I know that I won't.'

As Jarrett silently observed the bewitching planes and contours of Sophia's lovely face in the flickering firelight inside he was cheering—because she'd remarked that if she'd met him before she'd met her husband they might have been a good match. She might also have asserted that she wouldn't change her mind about entering into a relationship with him, but quite frankly that cut no ice. Because he wouldn't be deterred…not when he knew that it was the outcome he craved above all else—*even* above owning High Ridge.

And when it came to determination in achieving a goal…*any* goal…his ability to follow through and not be dissuaded was second to none.

'One day soon,' he said, 'I hope that you can tell me exactly what happened between you and your husband. I want to know what put that look of cold dread in your eyes that I sometimes glimpse. It's my opinion that you deserve to be free of whatever haunts you, Sophia. Not just for your own sake, but for Charlie's too.'

Curling her hair behind her ear, she left the ghost of a wan smile briefly curve her lips. 'Some hurts that we're haunted by are too deep to ever be free of,' she answered softly, 'but I *will* tell you my story. Not tonight, because it's getting late and I'm tired, but soon—I promise.'

'Fair enough… How about tomorrow afternoon?' Jarrett suggested boldly, somehow knowing that if they left the topic alone for too long she might again retreat into herself and not tell him anything. 'I'll bring my cricket bat and teach Charlie how to play, then afterwards you and I can talk.'

There was a very brief flash of concern in her mesmerising eyes, but then to his relief her expression softened. 'Okay. Come over tomorrow after lunch—around three o'clock. You can stay for tea.'

'Perfect.' He grinned. If he'd been on his own Jarrett would have punched the air with joy...

CHAPTER FIVE

'COME in. It's so good to see you!' Standing back to allow the tall fair-haired young man entry into the hallway, Sophia smiled up into eyes that reflected the same soft green hue as her own.

Her brother David hugged her hard, not hesitating to express his heartfelt love and affection. He was without a doubt pleased and happy to see her. He'd rung her on her mobile only a couple of hours ago, to tell her that he was driving down from Suffolk on his way to visit an antiques market in London and wanted to pay her a flying visit to see how she and Charlie were settling into the house—did she mind that it was at such short notice?

Of course she didn't.

Sophia simply felt blessed that she was able to renew their relationship after being separated for so long by the unhappy restrictions of her marriage. Tom had been so possessive of her that towards the latter months of his life he'd even banned David from visiting her. The only reason that her brother hadn't fought harder for the right to do so was because he'd feared the consequences for her and Charlie if he did.

'I've missed you, Sophia…I can't begin to tell you how much.' Holding her at arm's length, so that he could make a thorough reconnaissance of her face, her handsome sibling smiled a dazzling smile that had the look of a child on Christmas morning having just opened the gift he'd been hoping to receive above all others. 'You're looking really well…the best I can remember seeing you look for a long time. I'd almost forgotten how pretty you were! Did the two rooms I got ready for you work out all right? I'm sorry that I didn't have more time to make them a bit more welcoming.'

'They worked out just fine. After what I'd endured, trust me…a tent pitched in a field would have been welcome if no one had access to disturb me or try to control me and tell me what to do.'

They both knew who she was referring to with that comment, and some of the colour in David's face drained away a little. He dropped his hands down to his sides.

'I'm so sorry, Soph. So sorry that I didn't try and get you and Charlie away from him long before the bastard went and died.'

'Please don't beat yourself up about that. I know you must have been thinking of us. But the truth is the situation was a nightmare, with no easy solutions to bring it to an end. I know you would have done more if you could have. Besides, you had your wife and child to think of—and you know how vindictive Tom could be. I wouldn't have wanted you or your family to be at risk in any way. Look, let's not talk about this today, hmm?' She laid her hand on the soft suede of his jacket sleeve and lightly squeezed his arm. 'Let's just enjoy our time together knowing we've at last got the freedom to be brother and sister again without interference—agreed?'

He scraped his fingers through the cropped fair hair that highlighted his strong square-cut jaw and glanced back a little uncertainly into her eyes, as if debating whether anything he ever said or did could help take the sting out of the horrors of the past, no matter how much he wished that they could. 'Okay...I only want to do whatever makes you feel safe and secure again. God knows that's long overdue. Why don't you tell me how you and Charlie are doing? Where is he, by the way?'

'In the garden...he practically lives out there when the weather's fine. I'll call him in shortly to come and say hello to you.'

'As long as he's well and happy—that's the main thing. This place must seem like a veritable castle to him it's so big! You've certainly got your work cut out if you're planning on eventually renovating the place.'

'That's an understatement.' Sophia grinned. But then she frowned as she remembered something she'd badly wanted to address since being left the house by their relative—something that had been playing on her mind ever since she'd heard the news. 'Did you mind very much that Great-Aunt Mary left High Ridge to me instead of to us both?'

'Did I mind?' Her handsome brother was already shaking his head in disbelief. 'Are you mad? I was absolutely delighted. Especially when I knew that that poor excuse of a husband of yours had left you and Charlie practically destitute and I found out that you had to sell your home to pay off his debts. As for myself, I'm fortunate to have a place of my own as well as a good income with which to maintain it and to live on. Nothing could have pleased me more than to hear that some good fortune had come your way at last.'

Sophia's anxiety over the matter thankfully eased, to be happily replaced by a wave of the most profound relief. 'Thanks for that. I don't think I could have borne it if you'd been at all resentful. And, in answer to your question, Charlie *is* well and happy. He's starting his new school in a couple of weeks, and he's looking forward to making some new friends. I'm not doing too badly either, though it still feels a bit like I've been let out of jail. How are Lindsay and Oscar doing?'

'Oscar's seven going on sixteen!' David answered wryly. 'And if his current stroppy moods are anything to go by Lindsay and I will have our work cut out when he becomes a teenager, that's for sure'

'Why don't you come into the kitchen and we'll have a cup of tea and a chat? I was going to make some lunch for me and Charlie very soon— just something simple. You're welcome to join us if you're not in too much of a hurry to get to London?'

Even as she issued the invitation Sophia remembered with a jolt that Jarrett was paying her a visit after lunch, and that she'd promised to tell him the whole story of her bitterly unhappy marriage. She wouldn't put off the visit, but she'd rather her brother left before he arrived. All morning, whenever she'd reflected on seeing him again, she'd felt almost sick with nerves.

Yet underneath the nerves was growing a distinct sense of excited anticipation, and it was that pleasurable expectation that worried her *far* more than being judged on making such a terrible marriage and enduring it for so long, when she should have found the courage to get herself and Charlie away from the situation as soon as possible...*whatever* the threatened or imagined consequences.

Jarrett had hardly slept. He'd risen early and busied himself with inconsequential activities, like browsing the Sunday newspapers, surfing the internet and drinking enough coffee to raise a person from the dead, simply to kill the time before he could drive over to High Ridge Hall and see Sophia. *It was as though someone had put a spell on him.* He could hardly think about anything else but her beautiful face, and the realisation that he was a different man when he was in her company—a man who was far more in touch with his feelings than he usually managed.

The mere idea of being so vulnerable to a

woman would have normally had him running for the hills. God knew he'd had a lifetime of doing just that, fooling himself that long term relationships were best avoided because he didn't want to deal with the grief he might feel if things didn't work out. Losing his parents in a car accident when he was young had taught him that loving someone wasn't always enough to keep them by your side. Better to not risk being hurt, should that ever happen again. Yet what was happening to him now as far as Sophia was concerned was completely out of his control. And while it was undoubtedly frightening, it was also the most wonderful thing that he'd ever experienced.

Now, drawing up outside the familiar manor house, he reached over to the back seat of the car to collect the enormous bunch of flowers he'd brought for Sophia. They were all hand-picked from his own well-planted gardens. He and his gardener had walked the stone paths between the colourful beds together to select and cut them. Jarrett smiled to himself, shaking his head in bemusement as the heady floral perfume drifted up to him.

Even his gardener—the elderly but still sprightly Alfred—had winked knowingly up at him when he'd asked him to help choose some of the most beautiful blooms for a 'friend'. As the gnarled hands had reverently cut stalks with secateurs, the gardener had said, 'Your friend is a very lucky young lady indeed, Mr Gaskill. I hope she knows that.'

Stepping out onto the pavement, Jarrett walked up to the rusted iron gate that was positioned between tall hedgerows scattered with pink and white blossoms. It opened directly onto the house's path. Inside his chest, his heart was infused with optimism and hope for a good outcome to his visit—an outcome that would herald the start of what could be a genuinely meaningful relationship between him and Sophia Markham. But as he put his hand out to open the gate, up ahead the front door opened and a tall fair-haired young man stepped onto the stone porch with Sophia. His thoughts suspended in shock and surprise, Jarrett froze as he observed the man envelop the small slender brunette in a tight bearhug and pull her head down onto his chest. He then proceeded to stroke his hand lovingly over her hair.

A harsh breath that was akin to the aftermath of being punched exited his lungs. *She'd lied to him.* Above the white noise that drowned out all other sounds that was the thought that pounded Jarrett's brain. Was she even a widow, as she'd claimed? If she was, then she obviously hadn't wasted any time in finding herself a replacement for her husband.

Engulfed by jealousy and rage, he felt his heart thunder hard. When he saw Sophia step back to cup the man's face tenderly between her hands, and smile up at him as if he was infinitely dear to her, it became too much for him to linger there a second longer. His mind teeming with desperately furious thoughts about what an idiot he was to be taken in by her beautiful face and bewitching company, he turned away and strode quickly back to the car—the need to escape that hurtful, bitter scene was paramount. On the way, he deliberately let the lovely bouquet he'd brought her fall carelessly onto the ground, as though the carefully handpicked blooms were nothing but an unwanted and ugly bunch of weeds.

'Why didn't Jarrett come and teach me to play cricket today, Mummy?' her small son asked plaintively as Sophia tucked him into bed.

Her hand shook slightly as she smoothed it over the patterned eiderdown, thinking hard what to say. In truth, she'd begun to believe that Jarrett had reneged on his agreement to visit because he'd suddenly got cold feet. The thought was hard to bear after he'd been so kind the evening before, and as the day had worn on she hadn't been able to help becoming close to despondent when she'd realised he wasn't going to show.

He could have at least dropped a note through the letterbox to tell her that something else had come up. He could even have made up some not too hurtful excuse as to why he'd changed his mind, Sophia reflected. But could she blame him? After all, what man in his right mind would seriously contemplate taking on a woman like her? A woman who wore the battle scars of her bitter experience in her eyes every time she met anyone's glance?

It didn't matter that she'd resolved never to put herself in the path of such a dangerous liaison again—that she would stay alert and awake round anyone who had the slightest propensity to mistreat her. Somehow Jarrett Gaskill had got under her skin—even made her long for something she could never have.

Her self-confidence had already been shattered by the hard and lonely years spent with Tom, and her ability to trust had been severely tested—perhaps *beyond* repair. It had taken a huge leap of faith on her part even to invite Jarrett into the house, let alone contemplate deepening their association. She'd become used to assuming a shield as strong as toughened steel to fend off anyone who tried to get too close or pry into her business. Protecting herself and her son from harm or hurt had taken priority over everything, and rightly so. She should definitely take it as a warning that she'd dared to relax her guard round Jarrett so soon, only to be paid back by his letting her down.

Why had she done such a thing?

The answer came immediately. She'd risked trusting him because hope had started to stir in her heart that he was cut from a finer cloth than her husband, and now it hurt all the more that he'd disappointed her. It was a fruitless exercise, but Sophia couldn't help wondering *why* again. Was it because he'd concluded that she just wasn't worth the risk or the potential heartache?

'I don't know why he didn't come, my darling, I really don't,' she answered, tenderly stroking back her son's corkscrew curls from his forehead. 'Perhaps he wasn't feeling well. Anyway, I don't want you to worry about it, because I'm sure we'll find out what happened very soon. In the meantime, you've got your stay with Uncle David and Aunt Lindsay to look forward to. You're going to have so much fun, spending some time with your cousin Oscar, I'm sure. Now, get some sleep, my angel. You've had an exciting day, what with building a den in the garden and seeing your uncle again. I can see that you're tired. I love you so much, Charlie.' Affectionately brushing her lips against her son's soft cheek, Sophia got up from his bedside and moved across to the door.

'I love you too, Mummy...more than anybody else in the whole wide world!'

As she quietly closed the door behind her the distressing sting of tears pressed against her eyelids like a painful burning brand.

Jarrett had been in a foul mood all week. Each day he'd risen practically at dawn to seek refuge in work, and he lingered late in his office when he didn't have to—just to escape the mocking reality of his empty home. However desirable the executive-style house might appear from the outside, with its panoramic windows, the Ferrari, vintage Bentley and Range Rover parked on the drive outside the garage, and its landscaped gardens encompassing almost three acres of prime countryside, there was no getting away from the fact that inside it had suddenly become too cavernous and empty for him to tolerate being there on his own. With nothing but his despairing thoughts to keep him company, it had become a prison.

Even when his sister had rung to apologise for offending him with her remark about him wanting to get close to Sophia only so that he could buy High Ridge, he'd been too disheartened and impatient to forgive her. Beth's speculation about the woman he desired rankled even more now that he had discovered that she did indeed have secrets that she'd taken pains to conceal from him.

His mind couldn't seem to dislodge the disturbing image of her tender expression when she'd gazed up into her lover's eyes and gently cradled his face between her hands. Up until he'd witnessed that heart-knifing scene Jarrett couldn't deny that he'd been longing for Sophia to gaze up at *him* in a similar loving way one day soon. And, even though she'd so cold-heartedly deceived him, he couldn't totally kill that longing.

At least choosing to work even longer hours had helped ensure he wouldn't run into her by chance and perhaps be driven to express publicly his anger and disappointment at her deception. He imagined her soft husky tones explaining who the man was, and maybe a beseeching look in her green eyes that begged his understanding and forgiveness. *How in hell was he going to deal with that?*

About to climb out of the car and step onto his drive, he cursed vehemently, tunnelling his fingers furiously through his hair. At the same time the ominous sound of rumbling thunder made him glance up at the sky, to see the darkening grey dome above him turn to a dramatic blackened violet. Barely a few seconds later heavy rain began pelting everything in sight like indiscriminate machine gun fire.

The fresh string of curses that issued from Jarrett's lips was even more vehement than the first. Tugging his jacket collar up towards his ears, he hurriedly exited the car and slammed the door shut. *He'd be drenched long before he reached the front door.* Fine! It suited his already bleak mood to be soaked to the skin and made even colder in body, mind and spirit than he was already.

'Jarrett!'

For a frozen second he thought he'd imagined Sophia's voice calling out his name. But when he glanced over his shoulder towards the end of the drive he saw that his imagination *wasn't* working overtime. Her slim, rain-coated figure was huddled on the other side of the wrought-iron gates. Her hands were jammed into her pockets and her braided hair was plastered to her head by the violent downpour. Her lovely face was so pale that the exquisite cheekbones seemed to jut through the porcelain skin.

In spite of what she'd done to him Jarrett's heart slammed against his ribs, and in those arresting few moments his desire for her surmounted all doubt. He took a deep breath in to steady himself.

'What is it you want from me, Sophia? You'd better tell me quick, before we both drown in this monsoon!'

Through the deluge of heavily falling rain he saw her bite her lip and lift her sodden braids away from her face. 'Just tell me one thing. Why didn't you show up on Sunday? Charlie was so upset. You could have at least have had the decency to let us know you weren't coming.'

'I'm sorry I let your son down. I really am. But though I fully understand why *he* was upset, clearly *you* didn't suffer the same regret, did you?'

'What do you mean?'

'You know damn well what I mean!' He glared at her, clenching his fists down by his sides and shaking his head. 'You'd better come in. This is ridiculous. We can't talk out here'

He pressed a button on his keypad to open the electronic gates, refusing to contemplate for a moment that she might refuse his invitation to follow him inside and talk. *She owed him that much.*

Although her hair and outer clothing were clearly soaked, in no way did Sophia cut a forlorn figure. In fact, as she walked through the open gates towards him she held her head up high as if she didn't have a damn thing to hide.

He moved quickly towards the smart beech-wood front door. Although outside the rain pounded at the building with almost uncanny force, inside the light and airy hall it was suddenly as quiet as a church. Shrugging off his jacket and hanging the soaked garment on the coat rack inside the door, where it dripped into an umbrella stand, Jarrett impatiently stretched out his hand to take Sophia's coat. Seeing the hesitation in her glance, he bit back his impatience and trusted his expression was benign enough not to make her nervous. Even if she *had* lied to him, he would never descend to intimidation to vent his anger.

When she didn't remove her coat, he lowered his hand. 'Wait here. I'll go and get a towel for you to dry your hair.'

'Don't bother about that. Just answer the question I asked you outside and I won't take up any more of your valuable time.'

There was a hurt, resentful edge to her tone,

and Jarrett wrestled with the sense of injustice it provoked inside him. It beggared belief that she was acting so aggrieved when it was *her* that had played him for a fool.

'All right I'll tell you why you didn't see me. Although as a matter of fact I *did* call round.' Feeling the talons of what he believed was justifiable anger dig into him at the expression of surprise on her face, he slowly crossed his arms over his chest, praying that she wouldn't try and maintain her innocence to the point of embarrassing herself when she realised he knew the truth. 'I was about to open the gate when I saw you step outside the house with a man,' he said, low-voiced. 'A tall, fair-haired chap. Is he your lover, Sophia? Or perhaps he's the husband you told me had died?'

'What?' Her face had turned the colour of parchment. 'You say you called and saw me come out of the house with a man?'

'Yes, I did. I was about to open the gate when I saw him. Who was he? I don't want any lies. Just tell me the truth.'

Sophia's limbs were almost too weak to keep her upright for another second. The cold, damp material of her raincoat clung to her, making her shiver hard. She'd left the house in a hurry, unable to stand for a moment longer the torment of not knowing why Jarrett hadn't called round last Sunday. But it was the bitter disappointment and fury now reflected in his crystal blue gaze that made her tremble even more..

'For your information, I didn't consider telling you anything *but* the truth,' she insisted, and saw a muscle in the side of his strongly defined cheekbone flinch, as if denoting that he didn't believe her. 'The man who you saw me with is not my lover. He's my brother.'

Her companion's lightly tanned skin actually blanched, and she saw him swallow hard. 'Your *brother*?'

An icy drip of water slid down the back of her neck from her sodden coat collar, but her blood was pumping so hard through her veins that the heat it poured into her body right then meant that she barely even registered it. 'Yes, he's my brother. And if you'd had the guts and good manners to open the gate and walk in, instead of skulking outside and jumping to the worst possible conclusions, then I would have introduced you to him.'

'My God.'

'Now you know the truth, there's no need for me to hang around any longer.'

'Please wait. Look, I'm truly sorry. You can't know how much I mean that. I made a terrible mistake.'

'That's all that you can say? I thought you were a good man…a *fair* man. But then you go and shatter my illusions by behaving just like everybody else in this godforsaken place, with their small minds and unfair suspicions. I would have told you everything if you'd stayed. I see now what a bad error of judgement that would have been. Anyway, I am going to leave now, and I think it's best if we don't see each other again.'

Even as the words left her lips Sophia knew she didn't mean them. Having not set eyes on Jarrett for almost a week, she'd yearned to see him so badly that the image of his handsome face had seared itself onto her brain practically to the exclusion of all else. But she also knew it was unlikely she'd be able to trust him again, after he'd jumped to the wrong conclusion about David.

'Don't go.' He stepped towards her and stilled her escape by catching her hand and holding it. His expression mirrored his distress. 'At least give me the chance to make amends. You're right. I was a small-minded idiot not to give you the chance to explain who he was. But I was so intent on seeing you that I reacted like a jealous fool when I saw you with someone I thought must be a rival.'

'That's still no excuse for staying away without even contacting me to tell me why.'

'You're right. It isn't.' As he lifted one broad shoulder and dropped it again in a shrug a rivulet of rain slid down his sculpted cheekbone from his still wet hair. 'I suppose I thought the longer I stayed away, the longer I could delay hearing you tell me that there *was* someone else in your life after all.'

The tenor in his voice conveyed genuine regret, and in spite of her reservations Sophia sensed some of her anger and tension subside. Hearing Jarrett tell her that he'd acted like a jealous fool made her realise how much it must have meant to him to see her again that Sunday, and how shocked and disappointed he must have been when he'd believed she was seeing someone else.

He still hadn't released her hand, and it was as though an electrical current was shooting through it simply because his big palm enfolded it. 'There's nobody else.' She lifted her head, intensifying her gaze to emphasise the point. 'But that doesn't mean I'm looking for a relationship either.'

His lips split into a disarming grin. 'You know it's going to be my mission to make you change your mind about that?'

'By all means try. But don't say I didn't warn you when you fail.'

Letting go of her hand, he drove his fingers through his damp ebony hair. 'Will you still share what you were going to tell me before I made such a colossal fool of myself on Sunday? I honestly want to hear your story, Sophia. And before you say anything else, I'll make you a cast-iron promise that I won't share the content of what you tell me with another living soul.'

'Not even your sister?'

'Not even her.'

She saw from his unwavering stare that he meant it.

'By the way, where's Charlie?' he asked.

She gave him a brief smile. 'With my brother and his family. They've invited him to stay with them in Suffolk for a short break before he starts school. David has a son just a couple of years older than Charlie, and they haven't seen each other for a long time. I'm glad that he wanted to go, but I'm going to miss him like crazy.'

Just the thought of being without her precious child for even a *day* made Sophia feel tearful. They'd always had the strongest bond, but they'd become even closer since the shadow of Tom had no longer loomed over them.

Jarrett's glance was warmly reassuring. 'You'll

be fine,' he told her. 'I know you'll miss the little man, but you could probably do with a bit of a break too.'

'I suppose it's a good opportunity to get on with doing some work…both my photographic assignments *and* the house.'

The man in front of her looked thoughtful. Then with another warm smile he said, 'Why don't you let me hang up your coat? Then we'll go into the kitchen and have a hot drink.'

With fingers still icy-cold from the rain that had drenched her, Sophia slowly started to unbutton her damp raincoat.

CHAPTER SIX

THE hot mug of tea helped to dispel the chill that seemed to have seeped right through to her marrow.

Not since her father had Sophia known a man who knew his way confidently round a kitchen, and it had been an unexpected bonus to have Jarrett make the tea and then bring it to her at the table, along with an inviting plate of custard creams. As she'd watched his eye-catching physique garbed in a black fitted cashmere sweater and black trousers move with arresting masculine grace round the luxurious bespoke kitchen—a kitchen that was a million miles away from her own rather spartan one at High Ridge—Sophia hadn't been able to help but be transfixed.

Her heart was still thudding inside her chest because she'd at last found out why he hadn't turned up on Sunday. It had been the biggest shock to learn that he'd arrived just as her brother was saying goodbye and had immediately assumed that David was her *lover*. Although she'd forgiven him, it still hurt that he'd believed for even an instant that she was the kind of woman who would deceive him like that.

'Is your tea all right?'

Her host's arresting voice broke through her reverie. As he dropped down into the seat opposite her at the round glass-topped table, for a moment the close proximity of his arresting presence made it almost impossible for Sophia to think straight. His sexy but classy cologne made a devastating foray into her senses first. But then she met his gaze. His dark-lashed eyes were so blue that it was as if God had especially reserved the perfect portion of sunlit summer sky to make them. Entranced, Sophia hoped that the neutral expression she aimed for adequately concealed the effect he was having on her.

'It's perfect. Just the way I like it. Where did

you learn such a mundane but *vital* domestic task?'

'My sister always told me that the way to a woman's heart was through the perfect cup of tea.'

'Did she really?'

'No. I'm only joking.' His lips formed an unabashed grin. 'Living by myself, I've learned to do most things. I draw the line at wearing an apron, though. Wouldn't be at all good for my street cred if my family or friends were to see me in one.'

'Why don't you just pay someone to look after the domestic side of things for you?'

'Ah…' Jarrett knowingly tapped the side of his perfectly shaped aquiline nose. 'Now you're veering very close to discovering my Achilles' heel.'

'Which is?'

'Clearly you believe in living dangerously.' The lowered husky voice that came back to her made the tips of Sophia's breasts inside her bra surge and sting. 'Don't tell me, then.' She endeavoured to sound nonchalant when she was feeling anything *but*.

'I'm a boring perfectionist, I'm afraid,' Jarrett admitted wryly. 'I somehow always come round to thinking that I may as well do it myself rather than hire someone who won't live up to my standards.'

'You're a bit of a control freak, then?'

'That accusation is not unknown to me.' He took a sip of his beverage, then grimaced. 'But I hope I'm not controlling in a way that puts me in the category of typically macho male. With the right woman I'm sure I could learn to be a lot more flexible.'

His glance was sheepish, and too endearing for her to take umbrage with, and she lightly shook her head as if to break free from the spell he so effortlessly cast. 'It's entirely up to you how you conduct yourself. One thing puzzles me, though. This house and the expensive cars on the drive, plus the fact that you're not exactly ugly…women must view you as quite a catch. It makes me wonder why you're still single.'

'Clearly not *all* women think I'm such a catch. You're not particularly impressed by my wealth *or* my looks. I know I'm risking denting my ego even further by asking, but why is that, Sophia? I'm feeling a little insecure here, knowing that none of my supposed assets can entice you.'

Bravely she met his searching gaze, her mouth drying at the weight of hurtful memory that backed up inside her like a swelling wave, knowing that she could no longer let it recede. 'I was married to a man who had wealth and good-looks—and it was like being married to the *devil* himself,' she admitted softly.

'Why? What did he do?' Jarrett's eyes were wild for a moment—the very thought of any harm coming to her was abhorrent to him.

Glancing away, Sophia desperately tried to garner every ounce of courage she could find to continue. 'There's more than one way to skin a cat, as my dad used to say, and my husband knew them all. He was a virtuoso in the art of being cruel. Unfortunately it wasn't just *me* who bore the brunt of it.'

Her companion's sharp intake of breath was clearly audible. On his face, the shock that mingled together with disbelief was vivid too. 'You mean he hurt Charlie?'

'Not physically, thank God.'

She quickly moved her head from side to side, wishing they could talk about anything but *this*. However, she had promised her companion that she would tell him everything. She had never even shared the full extent of what she'd experienced at her husband's hands with her brother. To her mind, David had suffered enough, knowing that she lived with such a brute and that if he'd tried to take action to bring an end to her misery it might have made the situation worse for her and Charlie. There was no reasoning with a man like Tom Abingdon.

'Mental cruelty was his speciality,' she said out loud, 'and he could be as sulky and petty as a spoilt child. He regularly demanded that Charlie pay him more attention, because our son naturally came to me if he wanted or needed anything. He'd go ballistic at him for doing that. It was an affront to him that our boy needed his mother. After all, *he* was the one who was clever and educated—as he so often reminded me. He was the one with friends who admired and envied him, whereas I was a nobody. A picayune from a very average, nondescript family. He even told Charlie that I was a useless mother as well as a useless wife to him, and that they both deserved better. In a bid to prove it, he brought his mistress home.'

Sophia saw Jarrett's jaw slacken in disbelief and bit down heavily on her lip. 'I can see in your eyes that you're wondering why on earth I would put up with something like that if I had any self-respect at all.' Anger—defensive and bitter—crept into her voice. 'Well…perhaps you'll hold back your judgement until you hear the whole story. I hope that you will, because I'm *so* sick of being judged.'

Somehow she made herself continue. 'One evening when he brought this woman home—he'd been besotted with her for quite a while, I gather—he tried to convince our son that she would make a much better mother than me. She knew how to teach a boy to become a man, he said. She wouldn't turn him into some "namby-pamby Mummy's boy" like I was doing.'

She swallowed hard across the burning cramp in her throat. 'Tom thought he was justified in having affairs because after I'd had Charlie I locked him out of our bedroom. But I did that *because* he was always making eyes at other women, and when he didn't come home nights I knew he was messing around.' She freed a despairing sigh.

Jarrett gave her a quizzical look. 'He *let* you lock him out of the bedroom?'

Sophia's short burst of laughter was harsh. 'I think that was the first time I made him realise that I wasn't the gullible little schoolgirl he thought I would stay for ever when he married me. I was so furious with his behaviour that I didn't care if he hit me. I discovered it's a powerful thing to meet your fear instead of running away from it. But then he got back at me by other demoralising means. The worst thing of all was when he insisted on taking Charlie out for the day…away from my "despicable' influence", he used to say. I knew he'd be with his so-called friends. Friends who were as self-destructive and immoral as he was. I fought against him taking Charlie every time, and suffered not only verbal but sometimes physical abuse too for my protests.'

Taking a deep breath in at the dreadful memories that flooded back—at the humiliation and hurt of being hit and disparaged, along with her growing fear at the time that her son would grow up to be just like his father if she didn't find a way to get him away soon—Sophia laid her hand over her chest in a bid to calm her thudding heart.

As soon he saw the gesture, Jarrett moved across to the sink and poured some water into a glass tumbler. Returning swiftly, he pressed it into her hand.

Gratefully, she took a few sips and her companion moved back to his seat. Setting the glass down on a coaster, Sophia darted out her tongue to lick the moisture from her lips. Then she resumed her story. 'Leading up to the time when Tom died—his heart stopped beating one night in his sleep—Charlie was clearly being adversely affected by his father's behaviour. And why wouldn't he be? He was wetting the bed at night, having nightmares that made him scream out loud, and hitting me if I said no to something he wanted. I'm afraid it was making him ill.'

Jarrett scowled and looked disgusted. 'The man must have been absolutely deranged.'

'He was. He was addicted to everything that was harmful…alcohol, drugs, gambling, prostitutes. He had an utter lack of self-control and no self-respect whatsoever, and he didn't care who he contaminated—certainly not his wife and son. His death was a blessing, not just to me and Charlie…but to *him* too. I'm sure.'

'Why didn't you leave him long before it got so bad?'

Sensing an excruciating throb of guilty heat surge through her, Sophia abruptly left her seat and walked across the kitchen. There was an elegant glass wall cupboard full of pristine white

crockery and, catching sight of her ghostly pale
reflection in it, she quickly looked back to the
dark-haired man whose uncomprehending and
furious gaze seemed to burn right through to
the very core of her vulnerability. He was clearly
waiting for her explanation.

'I did leave him once. I went to a women's
shelter in a nearby town. It was only meant to
be a temporary measure. I'd planned to move
further away, but Charlie and I had only been
there barely a fortnight when Tom's father turned
up and demanded we leave. As well as being
a top QC, he comes from landed gentry…he's
a very powerful and influential man. He must
have brought the full weight of his powers down
on the women who ran the shelter, because by
the time they regretfully asked me to leave they
looked quite shaken. They told me he'd threatened to have the shelter shut down if they didn't
let me go, and that was the last thing that any
of us wanted. So I went back with him…back
to my husband. I wouldn't jeopardise the other
women's security by staying, no matter how des-

perate I was. Back at home, things didn't improve. And the situation wasn't helped by Tom's father. Whenever he visited us they had the most terrifying rows. He regularly accused Tom of being a disgrace to the family name, but worse than that he threatened to take Charlie away if he didn't pull himself together and change his behaviour. Ironic, really, when the man was even more of a bully than his son.'

She crossed her arms over her chest to contain the icy shudder that ran through her. 'It didn't even seem to cross his mind that I was Charlie's mother and would fight him tooth and nail on that. He believed that his son had married beneath him, so consequently he had very little regard for me. Tom's behaviour didn't change. He warned me he would take Charlie away from me himself if I told his father that his drinking, drug-taking and womanising had got worse. He was spending every penny we had on his destructive habits. He was pinning all his hopes on his inheritance. He said if I jeopardised his birthright by trying to leave then he would find me, come hell or high water. And then I would *really* see what he was capable of.'

Shaking her head in despair, Sophia lifted her now brimming eyes to Jarrett, incapable of holding back the emotional tide that swamped her. 'Both my husband and his father made it impossible for me to turn to anyone for help—even my brother. They blocked every avenue I could take. They didn't want me to talk to *anyone*. My father-in-law feared losing his reputation if anyone found out the truth about what was going on, and my husband was terrified he'd lose his inheritance. His debts escalated wildly—as I found out when he died. Because of their threats, because of my terrible fear that somehow they would snatch Charlie away from me if I *did* manage to escape—that was why I stayed in the marriage longer than I should have... *Not* because I wanted to, or because I had no self-respect, but because I honestly believed I had no choice.'

'You should have gone to the police...told them everything.'

'If I'd filed a report then they would have conducted an investigation. If Tom hadn't hurt me even more because I'd dared to do such a thing, then I've no doubt that his father would have done everything in his power to take Charlie away from me and make me pay for disgracing him and his son. Can you see why I couldn't do that? My son means everything to me…*everything*!'

'Don't cry, sweetheart…please don't cry.'

On his feet, Jarrett was by her side in an instant. Enfolding her in his arms, he pulled her head down onto his broad muscular chest. In the midst of her distress, a jolt of surprise ricocheted through Sophia. The wonderful sensation of being held so tenderly instantly made her feel warm and protected. She hadn't experienced such a feeling since she'd lived at home with her dad— before she'd met and married Tom Abingdon. But what surprised her most of all was the realisation that Jarrett's heart was beating as wild and as fast as her own beneath the soft wool of his luxurious cashmere sweater.

She lifted her face up towards him. 'Before my husband died I vowed to myself that I *would* find

a way to get Charlie and me out of that horrendous situation. I'd even started making discreet
enquiries about going abroad…somewhere far-
flung where Tom's father's influence carried no
weight. But then Tom died in his sleep…just like
that. When I found him he looked almost peaceful. It doesn't seem right somehow, does it? That
a man can put his family through such hell and
then abdicate all responsibility by simply dying?'

'I don't want to make you feel even more
upset—but why did you marry such a man in
the first place?'

Jarrett's big warm hand cupped her cheek as
he glanced intently down into her eyes. The
guilt she still suffered made Sophia struggle to
find adequate words to explain. 'I was young
and naive and flattered by his attention. He was
good-looking, funny and clever, and because he'd
been given everything on a silver spoon he was
supremely confident too. When it came to getting what he wanted he knew exactly how to go
about it, and when he decided that he wanted *me*
I was too young and stupid to see that I might

be walking into a trap. I was so dazzled by him that I relinquished every ounce of common sense I may have had. When he asked me to marry him I didn't even hesitate. Even when I started to hear rumours about his drinking and chasing women I told myself not to worry…that he would soon learn he'd made the right choice in making *me* his lifelong partner. I thought I could reform him, make him change some of his less attractive qualities when he saw what a good life we could have together.'

'How did you meet him?'

'I went to school with his younger cousin, and I met him at a party at her house.' Feeling suddenly uncomfortable beneath Jarrett's intense scrutiny, she removed his hand from her cheek and glanced away. 'No doubt I was easy prey. I was only eighteen—hardly a woman of the world. I'd just got into studying photography, and I wanted to go on to university. Meeting Tom put a stop to all that. It wasn't as though nobody warned me. My dad told me early on to cool things off and not rush into anything. But I was deaf to his advice. My husband-to-be even managed to fool *him* into thinking his intentions were good… that he loved me and wanted to take care of me. In the beginning I believed it, too. But it didn't take long for my fiancé's true nature to surface. I thank God that my dad didn't live to see what he put me through.'

The silence that pervaded the room after she'd finished speaking felt like a smothering blanket, and Sophia wanted to escape into the open air. Moving out of the intimate circle of Jarrett's protection, she lifted her glance to stare forlornly out of the window at the still pounding rain. She shivered.

'I'd better go. I'm trying to convert one of the downstairs rooms into a darkroom, and there's a lot to do. I have to get on. Thanks for the tea… and for listening.'

'Don't go. It can't have been easy to share what you've just told me. It was very brave. It's only natural that you might be feeling vulnerable and exposed. I made you a promise that I wouldn't share your confidences with anyone, remember?

I want you to know that you can trust me, Sophia. I would never harm you or Charlie.' Catching her hand, Jarrett gently impelled her towards him. 'You've been through a terrible ordeal,' he acknowledged huskily, 'but given time things will slowly but surely get better—believe me. This is a new start for you and your son. Your husband is dead, Sophia…he can't hurt you or Charlie any more.'

'What about his father? Why do you think I reacted the way I did when you came up to me that day by the stream? After Tom died I had to sell the house to pay off his debts, and his father suggested that Charlie and I move in with him instead of finding somewhere else to live. Can you imagine it? The thought filled me with absolute horror. I had to run away so that he wouldn't try and force me. That day, when you first saw me, I thought you were someone he'd hired to come and find me and snatch Charlie. If he ever finds out where I am he could—he might—'

'Hey…'

Jarrett drew the pad of his thumb down over

her cheek, and the look in his intense blue eyes along with the enticing flare of heat that his touch instigated inside her made Sophia sway a little closer towards him.

'Stop scaring yourself. You and Charlie are safe now,' he told her. 'I'll do everything in my power to make sure of that.'

'Why? Why would you do that for me?' The lid she'd tried so hard to keep firmly shut down on her emotions when she was with other people suddenly flew open, and she couldn't stop the slow track of scalding tears that started to spill down her face.

'You don't really need to ask me that…do you?'

His carved masculine mouth formed a knee-trembling smile that could melt a heart of stone, and although bruised and battered Sophia's heart was neither stony *nor* hard. She was ripe for a little tenderness, even though she'd sought to arm herself against it.

No further reflection was necessary as Jarrett laid his lips over hers in a kiss that started off on a slow-burning simmer and then quickly turned into a conflagration of passion and need. Again and again she gasped breathlessly into his mouth, needing to taste him, needing to feel the ravenous demand of his warm lips and hot tongue, meeting it with her own helpless craving, almost swooning with pleasure as his big hands dived into her hair and freed her still damp plaits. In response, her arms wound themselves round his lean hard middle to keep her steady.

The realisation that hit her like a tidal wave was that her sexual need hadn't been completely deadened by her husband's cruel behaviour, as she'd believed. His cutting taunts and profligate behaviour had killed her desire very quickly once they were married. By the time she'd learned she was pregnant with Charlie the mere idea of her husband's hands coming anywhere *near* her body had been like agreeing to imbibe poison. Now, with Jarrett, she felt like a neglected flower in a shaded part of the garden that had unexpectedly caught a shower of glorious summer rain just in the nick of time. If he had wanted to become more intimate with her there and then Sophia

would have let him. Her usually highly main-
tained defences had been demolished by that first
exquisite contact with his lips and the sensation
of his body pressing hungrily against hers. He
made her feel like a real woman again.

It was Jarrett who poured the first drops of ice-
cool water on the fire they'd made. Breaking off
their passionate kiss with a rueful smile, he held
her gently at arm's length, and she knew that
the sound of his fast and heavy breathing and
the look of stunned pleasure on his face easily
matched her own.

'As much as I desire you—and it must be obvious to you by now that I do—I won't take
advantage of you when you're clearly feeling vulnerable,' he asserted, his glance flicking concern-
edly over her face. 'When you're feeling calmer,
and know what you want without your thoughts
and feelings being clouded by emotion…then—
if you decide that's what you want—we can have
a more intimate relationship.'

Her heart was thudding so hard inside her chest
that Sophia couldn't get an immediate grip on her

emotions. Humiliation and shame slammed into her that she'd so stupidly exposed her need and vulnerability to Jarrett. Would he think it was no wonder that she'd ended up with a brute like her husband when she was clearly so desperate for love and affection…for *sex*?

Twisting out of his arms, she shakily rubbed her face dry of tears. 'Thanks for keeping a level head when I was clearly losing mine. I appreciate it. Now I'd better go. I have things to do at home. Like I said—I've started to convert a room into a darkroom to print my pictures and I really need to get on with it.'

'Sophia?'

'Yes?' The command in Jarrett's tone ensured her feet stayed firmly rooted to the spot when her preference was to escape as quickly as she could, so that she could go home and lick her wounds in private and examine why she had so eagerly let down her guard around him.

'I *want* you… Make no mistake about that. But it's not just sex that I want. What I want most of all is a relationship with you. I'd like to start by taking you out to dinner tonight.'

'I don't think that I—'

'Don't turn away from me. It's time you returned to the land of the living and started to enjoy life again.'

'The concept of enjoying my life feels like a million miles away right now,' she confessed quietly as she ventured to meet his piercing gaze.

'Well, maybe you can start by at least entertaining the thought. And by agreeing to go out to dinner with me tonight.'

The tumult inside Sophia started to subside a little, so that she was at last able to think more clearly. After Tom she'd been certain that she would steer clear of men—particularly *handsome* men—for the rest of her life.

With a trembling hand she brushed back the long waving hair that clung damply to the sides of her face. 'All right. I'll go out to dinner with you tonight. Satisfied?' she added with a touch of feistiness. Because although she wanted more than anything to go out to dinner with Jarrett she had to be careful not to seem too eager.

'After *that* kiss?' His face assumed an exaggeratedly pained expression. 'Not by a long chalk, sweetheart. Not when I think I've just discovered the true meaning of the word frustration!'

'You were the one who put a stop to it.'

'Very true.' A muscle hitched in the side of his sculpted cheekbone, and this time his expression was deadly serious. 'But I'm glad that I did. I want to get to know you, Sophia. I want you to get to know *me*. Isn't that how all good relationships are meant to start out? With friendship?'

She stared. The concept was alien to her...that a man and a woman could be *friends* before they were lovers.

CHAPTER SEVEN

IN THE softly lit restaurant, with candlelight flickering between them, at the beautifully laid corner table that he had specifically reserved, Jarrett formed his hands into a steeple and rested his chin on it to study his companion more closely.

It wasn't just the muted lighting and candlelight that rendered her features beautiful. It was a face that he could never imagine growing tired of looking at. Just one glance into eyes the colour of new-mown summer grass with sweeping chestnut lashes was enough to kindle a lifelong fascination. But it didn't hurt that Sophia's other features were equally compelling—from the small, elegant nose, the strongly defined pretty mouth, right down to the gentle cleft in a firm chin that denoted an uncommon strength of character and resolve. And, by God, she must have had to employ both of those attributes in spades during a marriage that had surely been made in hell.

He was still reeling at what she had told him. The truth had turned out to be much worse than he'd anticipated. The thought of her suffering at the hands of the sort of man her husband had been was enough to make a peaceable man like himself commit violence. In his opinion Tom had done her and Charlie a favour by dying suddenly like that. Still, it bothered Jarrett that Sophia would probably carry the psychological wounds of that terrible experience for the rest of her life.

That was why he had gently held her off in the midst of that incredible kiss they'd shared. He didn't want her to feel as if he was taking advantage of her in any way, even if his decision to cool things down a bit had been one of the hardest things he'd ever done. Now he planned to woo her properly...to let her know that he would put respect for her feelings, needs and wants above his own desires. He'd waited a long time for the right woman to come into his life, and Sophia was already too important to him to scare her off with any kind of rash move. You didn't rescue a bird with a broken wing and expect it to fly again without tending to it first, without allowing it time to heal.

'What are you thinking about, I wonder?' Sophia smiled, breaking into his thoughts.

'I was thinking about you.' There was a helpless, smoky catch in his voice.

'Boring subject…been there, done that. Earlier today, as a matter of fact—remember?'

She made a face and for a moment the child in her surfaced—a child who had been unbearably wounded. It made Jarrett's heart constrict. It was becoming clear to him that she went on the defensive at the least provocation. He didn't doubt her bitterly unhappy marriage had ripped into her sense of safety.

Leaning forward a little, he caught her gaze. 'How could you think yourself boring when the whole village is buzzing with speculation about you? You're not like anybody else round here… And although people are naturally suspicious because you're an unknown quantity, they're also envious.'

'You should know by now that they have nothing to be envious of. Besides, do you *think* I want that kind of attention? I'd rather live like a hermit in a cave. All I want is to be able to go about my business unnoticed and be like everybody else. Just to be ordinary. I'm not asking for the world. I have the same aspirations as most women round here, I'm sure… To be a good mother, be well paid for the work that I do, and to have a comfortable and affordable home. I love High Ridge, but I'd be a liar if I said that it doesn't keep me awake nights wondering if I haven't bitten off more than I could chew because I'm living in a house straight out of one of Dickens's novels!'

Jarrett smiled, wondering if she had any idea how beautiful she was in her simple wrap-around blue jersey dress, with her long chestnut hair glossy as dark fire as it flowed down over her slender shoulders. 'Those are reasonable and commendable aspirations indeed,' he answered thoughtfully. 'Except that I'm perturbed you haven't included the desire for a meaningful and happy relationship on your list. I was hoping you might include that one.'

Sophia's returning gaze was steady. 'Maybe that's because past experience has demolished all the optimism I once had.'

He was still soberly absorbing this comment when two smartly dressed waiters arrived with their food. The Italian restaurant Jarrett had driven them to was about ten miles from the village, deep in the heart of the surrounding countryside. The chances of bumping into anybody local were slim, and he'd hoped that might help Sophia to relax. Glancing down at the pasta dishes they'd selected from the menu, he didn't think either he or his companion would be disappointed with their choices. Not if the tasteful presentation and delicious aroma that wafted tantalisingly beneath his nose was anything to go by. And he knew the food was particularly good here because he'd eaten there on the odd occasion with his sister.

His stomach growled. The only sustenance he'd

imbibed all day was a slice of nearly burnt toast and a cup of strong black coffee at breakfast. In fact his appetite *and* his sleep had been poor all week, due to his belief that Sophia was seeing another man.

'Let's eat, shall we?' he suggested lightly, giving her a broad smile as their attentive waiters left them alone again. 'I don't know about you, but I could eat the proverbial horse!'

'So, not only don't you have someone to clean for you, you obviously haven't succumbed to hiring a cook either?' Picking up her fork, Sophia expertly twirled some strands of spaghetti round it, guiding it into place with her spoon.

For a moment Jarrett was too transfixed by the sight to even think about satisfying his own appetite. She somehow managed to make the most commonplace actions look sexy, he mused, as a pleasant buzz of heat infiltrated his insides, 'Are you putting yourself forward for the job? Because if you are then I'll happily forego the interview and appoint you straight away.'

She moved her head to indicate no. 'I won't

consider it right now, because I need to put my energies into my photography, but ask me again in a month or two when the coffers aren't exactly spilling over with coin and I might accept.' She popped a forkful of pasta with its accompanying fragrant sauce into her mouth and squeezed her eyes shut in a demonstration of unrestrained pleasure. 'Mmm…' she groaned. 'This is really, *really* good'

Jarrett almost let his fork clatter back onto the table. The look on her face was straight out of a candid scene from an erotic movie. Helplessly shifting in his seat as an arrow of flame zeroed straight into his loins, he suddenly found it wasn't food that he was hungry for.

'Aren't you going to eat?' Sophia asked innocently. 'I thought you were starving?'

He cleared his throat. 'I am. I'm afraid I just got a little distracted.'

'Oh.' She brushed off the comment with a careless shrug, but nonetheless he saw the swathe of hot pink that swept into her cheeks.

Feeling undeniably pleased, Jarrett watched

her tuck into her meal for a few seconds longer before hungrily attacking his own.

By the time coffee arrived Sophia was feeling much more relaxed and at ease. Tonight, in this lovely restaurant, she was like any other diner enjoying the company of her date, and nobody either knew or cared about her painful past. That gave her a sense of freedom and autonomy that she'd long craved.

Adding some cream to her coffee, she stirred it in, and when she looked up again Jarrett was studying her, an enigmatic smile lifting the corners of his mouth. A frisson of intense pleasure rippled through her as she recalled his urgent passionate kisses just a few short hours ago. There was no doubt in her mind that the man could win a trophy for his ability to kiss a woman and render her weak with instantaneous desire. In fact, there was so much about him that was wonderful that it was hard to fathom why he hadn't already met and married someone, Sophia mused.

'My turn to ask what *you're* thinking,' he remarked, just as her mind was in the middle of listing the qualities of his that she found the most appealing and attractive.

She smiled with a guilty blush. 'I was remembering that I once asked you why you were still single and you didn't really give me an answer. Have you ever had a long-term relationship?'

'No.' He shifted a little uncomfortably in his seat, settled again, then paused to take a sip of his strong black coffee.

Sophia was intrigued by his apparent reticence. 'Why not?' she asked bluntly.

'I guess up until recently I've never felt the desire to commit to anyone. No doubt there are many people who would think that's extremely selfish. My sister has despaired of me from time to time,' he said candidly, shrugging his shoulders. 'Don't get me wrong,' he added quickly, seeing her frown, 'I don't play the field…nothing like that. It's just that I've never met anyone that I wanted to be with for more than a few dates. And I've devoted most of my time to building my business.'

With a little flare of satisfied heat warming her

insides at the realisation that he'd been referring to her when he'd stated that 'up until recently' he'd never felt the desire to commit to anyone, Sophia leaned forward a little, unconsciously inviting more candid revelations about his feelings and his life. 'And what *is* your business, Jarrett?'

'In simple terms, I buy and sell land.'

'Locally, you mean?'

His arresting smile was modestly wry. 'All over the world,' he confessed.

'Goodness…no wonder you haven't had time for romantic relationships. Such a global undertaking must surely demand a huge amount of time and energy? How will you manage things if you ever *do* settle down with someone?'

She almost held her breath as she waited for his answer, wishing that it didn't suddenly matter quite so much as it did.

His returning glance was completely frank. 'It's fortunate that I have several very competent and skilled people working for me, so it wouldn't be a problem to delegate a little more in order to free up more time. Especially if I'm ever lucky enough to have a family.'

The unexpectedly revealing comment had the effect of silencing the next question that hovered on Sophia's lips and it made her heart gallop. Reminding herself to get a grip, and not to let her hopes run away with her, she unconsciously added another lump of brown sugar to her coffee and took a deep sip. It was far too sweet and she couldn't help grimacing.

Jarrett laughed, and Sophia blushed to the roots of her hair when she realised he had seen her sour-faced expression.

'I was wondering if you usually made a habit of putting five lumps of sugar in your coffee. I surmised that you clearly just had a very sweet tooth,' he teased.

'I'm afraid I lost count of how many I put in,' she murmured, colouring hotly.

'I'll order you a fresh cup.' About to beckon a waiter, Jarrett hesitated when Sophia reached out and touched his hand.

'Please don't,' she said earnestly. 'It would

probably keep me up all night anyway, and I need my sleep.'

'In that case I'll pay our bill and we'll go.'

Brushing back her hair from the side of her face, she nervously let her eyes meet his as she wondered what the protocol was these days on dating a man if he'd bought a woman a meal. *Was he going to expect much more than a goodnight kiss?*

A short while later, as they were sitting in the car in the impressive shadow of High Ridge, Sophia turned to her handsome companion and sighed. 'So there really hasn't been anyone you've been serious about in the whole of your romantic history?'

'That's right,' Jarrett answered. A thread of anxiety rippled through him that she might not believe him—that she might think he was just making it up to pique her interest.

'And you've never been lonely? Being on your own, I mean?'

The question made Jarrett smile. He knew perfectly well what she was asking him. 'If by lonely you mean have I ever felt the need for some fe-male company to share my bed, then, yes. I have.'

'And presumably there's been no shortage of takers?'

Even in the dimly lit interior of the car, her blush was endearingly delightful. From the roots of his hair to the tips of his toes, Jarrett's whole body tightened. 'Can we talk about something else?' he suggested lightly. 'For instance, are you going to invite me in for a coffee? I know you implied that too much caffeine keeps you awake, but I wouldn't say no to another cup if you're of-fering.' He knew his smile was boyishly hopeful.

Sweeping her hair behind her ear, Sophia was suddenly wary. 'Can we do that another time, maybe? I really am feeling rather tired tonight.'

'Why didn't you mention that earlier?'

'Because I was feeling fine then…it's only just hit me now we've arrived home. By the way, I've really enjoyed our evening together and the lovely meal. Thank you. It was so nice to be taken out to dinner. I can't remember the last time I did such a normal thing.'

'It was my pleasure. My hope is that we'll have many more evenings like this together. Are you okay?' he asked, frowning. The wary look hadn't retreated, he saw.

'Yes, I'm fine. A good night's sleep will sort me out, I'm sure.'

'I'll walk you to your door, then.'

'There's no need...thanks all the same.'

Sophia was already taking her keys out of her purse. As she glanced up again, Jarrett saw she appeared to be thinking hard about something.

'Do you still see any of the women who kept you company when you were lonely?' she quizzed him.

He might have known she wouldn't let him off lightly. She was behaving like every other woman who had the bit between her teeth about something. But in Sophia's case her need to know about this particular facet of his past was entirely justified, he thought—because she knew only too well the pitfalls of being with someone who couldn't be relied upon except to *hurt* her.

'No, I don't. I already told you I never dated

anyone for very long, but neither did I cold-heart-edly desert them. When we parted it was always mutual. The kind of women I saw were usually from the corporate world, as time-poor as me be-cause they were immersed in their careers, want-ing to make a name for themselves. Having a romantic relationship was never going to be top of their list of priorities.'

There had been one liaison where the woman in question had got a little bit too attached to the idea of deepening her association with him, Jarrett recalled wincingly, but he had told her as diplomatically and as kindly as possible that he couldn't consider it. She hadn't guessed that he was holding out for the woman of his dreams, and he wondered if she would have been surprised that he secretly harboured such a romantic ideal.

'Did you ever want more than just a mutu-ally satisfying fling with anyone in particular?' Sophia asked, just as though she'd read his mind.

He heard the slight condemnation in her voice and flinched inwardly. 'No, I didn't,' he admit-ted, low-voiced. 'And I don't want you to think that's because I'm some kind of devil-may-care playboy, because I'm not. The truth is I just never met anyone I fell for in that way. But that doesn't mean I haven't had a desire to. To fall in love, I mean.' He hardly knew how he kept his hands off of her as he said this, because she was becoming more irresistible and important to him every time he saw her.

Like now, when her face was so bewitchingly illuminated by the gentle rays of moonlight drifting in through the windscreen.

The smooth skin between her brows puckered in thought. 'I'm sure if it's meant to happen it will,' she commented, and then, leaning towards him, dropped a light kiss at the corner of his mouth.

A purely *chaste* kiss, Jarrett thought in frustration. Every masculine instinct he had clamoured for him to haul her into his arms and kiss her *properly*…to taste and ravish her mouth in the way that he yearned to do…to run his hands down over her lithe, beautiful body and build up a storm—a storm that he'd sensed had been brewing between them ever since he had first set eyes on her.

Yet he couldn't bring himself to succumb to such a raw, elemental need when the woman he desired was still wrestling with so many fears from her past. He would just have to learn to be patient.

Already out of the car, Sophia dipped her head to give him a smile. Her long hair fell softly around her face and framed it. 'If you want to drop round tomorrow some time and have coffee then I'd be glad to see you,' she said.

His relief was off the scale. For a moment there he'd worried that she might put him off indefinitely.

'What time?'

'Don't you have to work?'

'Yes, but tomorrow I'm working from home… How about eleven o'clock?'

'Eleven is fine. I'll see you then.'

Jarrett didn't respond with goodnight or goodbye. He merely gave her a brief nod. He guessed he wanted to avoid any reference to the fact that they were going to be parted—even if it *was* only until tomorrow...

A devastating nightmare had shocked Sophia awake. The icily threatening quality of the dream disorientated her, and for a moment or two she was completely unaware of where she was or even her own name.

Breathing hard, she sat up and swung her legs over the side of the bed. It jolted her to realise that she wasn't back in the expensive London house she'd once shared with Tom Abingdon, and neither was this her bed. She hardly remembered electing to sleep on Great-Aunt Mary's threadbare old couch, but now it came back to her. When she'd finally decided to turn in—just like on the previous three nights—it had hit her that she was all alone in the house *without* Charlie. It was too hard to sleep in her own bed when on the other side of the room her son's endearing little cabin-bed with its Paddington Bear quilt was empty, and above her the rest of the cavernous rooms were full of imagined ghosts that her imagination was only too eager to make real.

The fire that she'd left alight in the grate to keep her warm during the night was down to a few glowing embers, and the large stately room she'd been sleeping in was now so cold that it frosted her breath.

In the horrible nightmare that had visited her she'd been running barefoot through eerily menacing dark woods, with Tom chasing after her, threatening all kinds of dire consequences when he caught up. When the white-hot rage that he was still tormenting her had suddenly spilled over, giving Sophia the courage to turn and face him, the cruel face that had gaped back into her eyes hadn't been her deceased husband but his *father*…

A chill and queasy sensation lodged like congealed porridge in the pit of her stomach and made the inside of her mouth dry as sand. Reaching for the glass of water she'd left nearby on a table, she gulped the contents down. Before she finished the drink, the hot tears burning at the backs of her eyes were streaming in an unchecked flow down her face. She hadn't even undressed. She was still wearing the blue wraparound dress she'd worn out to dinner with Jarrett.

With stoic determination she scrubbed away the moisture streaking down her face with the heel of her hand. Just the thought of him sent a tropical heatwave sweeping through her blood and made her ache almost beyond bearing to see him again. And, for a blessed few moments even the memory of his reassuring presence drove out the cold and fear that gripped her. Simply recollecting his sculpted handsome face, haunting blue eyes and the richly sensual quality of his mesmerising voice was enough to make her yearn to have him appear. Not only was he the most attractive man she had ever seen, to Sophia's mind his best asset was his unquestioning ability to be kind. She'd seen plenty of evidence of that. Jarrett epitomised the very best of masculinity, where her deceased husband had epitomised the *worst*.

With all her heart she wished she could turn back the clock and invite him in for coffee, instead of walking into this lonely old house on her own. But her emotions had been in a distressing state of turmoil after her revelations to him about her marriage, and she'd feared she had told him too much. Confessing the details of her personal horror story had left her feeling uncomfortably exposed, and fear of Jarrett's unspoken judgement had made her want to distance herself from him for a while.

If only she hadn't succumbed to that painful impulse so quickly, she thought now. If she hadn't, he might still be here...

Jarrett had lain down on his bed fully clothed, thinking hard about the evening he'd just spent with Sophia. His mind simply refused to let him dwell on any other subject. It had done his heart good to see her tuck into her meal with such enjoyment, and he wondered how many meals she'd left uneaten or barely touched because she'd been consumed by the threat of harm her malicious ex-husband regularly seemed to have menaced her with?

His hands curled into fists down by his sides. He made himself think about something far less likely to arouse his fury. Apart from her undoubted beauty, there was so much that he admired about this lovely woman. For instance her ability to be brave in the face of the most horrendous adversity and not lose hope. Even now she was putting on a brave face, because her little son was away from home staying with his uncle and she was spending her nights at High Ridge alone.

Cursing out loud, because that particular thought was apt to inflame him and rob him of his sleep entirely, Jarrett got up, quickly shed his clothes, then got back into bed again, dragging the duvet up over his head to block out any disturbing glimpse of light. Then he turned his face into the pillow and willed sleep to rescue him from the too tempting images of Sophia that his mind seemed determined to taunt him with...

Jarrett wake up...you must wake up. I need you!

Sophia's voice—urgent and low—was right against his ear, shockingly stirring him from the deep, dreamless slumber that he'd fallen into. Immediately turning on his side towards her, Jarrett's heart hammered hard. Feeling as if he'd been cruelly cheated of the one thing that he longed for above all else when he realised the space beside him was empty, he reached towards the bedside lamp, almost knocking it over in his haste for illumination. Impatiently he switched it on. As light flooded the room, he sat up, scrubbing the sleep from his eyes with his knuckles.

The sound of her voice had been so *real*. Even more disturbing to his peace of mind was that it had sounded so frightened—*desperate*, even. Was she in trouble? *I need you*, she'd cried. Had that bastard of a father-in-law discovered her whereabouts and was right now threatening her?

Not even taking time to dwell on the sense of the action he intended, or be remotely concerned that it was the dead of night, Jarrett rushed into the dressing room adjacent to his bedroom, grabbed a pair of jeans and a sweatshirt from out of the bank of mirrored wardrobes that contained his clothes and quickly dressed. Returning to the bedroom, he pushed his feet into the pair of loafers he'd left by the bed, then grabbed the leather jacket he'd thrown onto a chair and hurriedly exited the room as though the hounds of hell themselves were snapping hungrily at his heels...

CHAPTER EIGHT

THE sudden thumping on the front door reverberated warningly through the house like the violent rumble of thunder heralding a storm. Clutching the folds of her dress anxiously to her chest, Sophia's blood turned to ice. *Who on earth would bang on her door like that in the middle of the night unless something was terribly wrong?*

Her thoughts naturally flew to her son. But surely if something untoward had happened to Charlie, her brother would have notified her with a phone call first? He wouldn't just turn up out of the blue and knock her door down! The next fear following close on the heels of the first one was that her father-in-law had found her and was waiting outside to confront her with a demand to see his grandson…to take him away from her. *What if he'd brought help with him to do just that?* She wouldn't put it past him to hire a couple of heavy-set thugs to accomplish what he was too cowardly to accomplish himself.

When she rose to her feet a surge of adrenalin pumped through her veins, rendering her almost too weak to stand. Quickly slipping her feet into the plain black leather pumps she'd worn to dinner, she stole a cursory glance at the fire now blazing brightly in the grate, thanks to the fresh ash log she'd added, and on the spur of the moment grabbed one of the heavy iron tongs in the stand beside it. Squeezing her eyes shut tight for a moment, she murmured a quick heartfelt prayer beneath her breath, then left the room to step out into the dark, cavernous hallway that led to the front door.

The porch light there had automatically come on, and she nearly fainted with fright at the sight of the tall shadow that loomed up behind the decorated glass panels.

'Sophia! Sophia, are you there? It's me, Jarrett.'

'Oh, my God.' Her reaction was as though someone had careened into her back with a battering ram. Her body felt weak and winded all at the same time.

Trembling hard, but this time with relief instead of stark cold fear, she laid the heavy iron tongs carefully down on the floor, glad to be free of their threatening weight now that she knew that she wouldn't have to employ them in self-defence. But her heart still pounded at the realisation that her night-time visitor was Jarrett... the man whose presence she'd been desperately longing for ever since she'd decided not to invite him in for coffee.

With fumbling fingers she undid the latch and the bolts at the top and bottom of the door. By the time the cool night air rushed in to greet her and she came face to face with her visitor Sophia hardly had the strength to hold herself upright. The shock she'd received at the pounding of the door had robbed her of every ounce.

'Are you okay? Tell me!'

Jarrett's face looked pale, haunted almost...as if he too had received the most disturbing shock.

The dim porch light highlighted the hard cobalt glitter of his mesmerising gaze.

Fastening his hands round her slim upper arms, he stared down into her face as if to make an urgent assessment of her state of mind. 'I heard you call out my name as if you were right there beside me. I wasn't dreaming, Sophia…your voice was as real as can be and you sounded distressed.'

'What did I say?'

'You said…you said, "I need you."'

Had her longing been so powerful that it had transcended time and space and transmitted itself straight to Jarrett?

But even before he'd confessed what he had heard Sophia had already been overwhelmed by the heat and solidity of his reassuring male body, and she couldn't help breathing out a heartfelt sigh as she gazed steadily up into his eyes. 'How strange that you heard that. It's true. I *do* need you, Jarrett. I had the most terrible nightmare. I dreamt that Tom and his father were coming after me. I haven't had a dream like that for a long time, and it was even harder to bear after such a nice evening. It really shook me up.'

Her legs buckled a little with the force of emotion that swept through her at the memory of the distressing dream and also at Jarrett's timely but altogether unexpected appearance...all because he'd had some kind of psychic intuition that she needed him.

Her handsome visitor didn't hesitate to catch her as her balance faltered, and he lifted her up high into his arms to hold her safely against his chest as though she weighed nothing. Then he carried her into the dimly lit hallway. Its scant illumination came from the warm light that drifted out through the open drawing room door at the end of it. Inside, Sophia had left one small lamp burning, and the fire she had lit to chase away the chill of her nightmare still emitted a welcoming bright blaze.

Kicking the front door shut with the heel of his boot, Jarrett made a beeline for the softly lit room. Once inside, he headed straight for the old-fashioned couch where Sophia had left her quilted eiderdown to drape over her as she slept, and dropped her carefully down onto a cushion, still cradling her in his arms.

'I'm glad you lit the fire. The warmth and light will help—especially after that nightmare,' he said with gentle authority, his fingers tenderly brushing back some long skeins of silky chestnut hair that had partially drifted over her face.

His touch was *divine*. Straight away Sophia sensed a delicious melting sensation in the nether region of her stomach. The scent from his body was sexy, warm and compelling, and the tough denim of his jeans couldn't disguise the iron hardness of his strong, muscular thighs. He'd already intimately acquainted her with how strong he was, making light work of lifting her up into his arms and carrying her, and since he'd swept her up against his chest even the icy tentacles of the dreadful nightmare that had visited her had lost most of their power to hold her in their chilling grip. Right now the only thing that was unsettling her—but in a *good* way—was Jarrett.

'I'm sorry if I frightened you, banging on your

door like that, but when I thought you might be in danger I had to come to you.' The palm of his big warm hand settled against her cheek and tenderly cupped it.

'I'm glad that you did.' Her soft voice was a little breathless.

'Do you want to tell me about the dream? It can sometimes help to dispel the memory if you talk about it rather than just bottle your feelings up inside.'

'I'd rather not, if you don't mind. I'm already feeling better because you're here...honestly.'

A muscle flinched in the side of his unshaven cheek. 'I'm glad about that. I really am. But you must know that sooner or later you're going to have to confront this bully of a father-in-law of yours, or else he'll be intimidating you for the rest of your life...and maybe Charlie's too.'

'I know—and you're right.' Sophia agreed with a sigh. 'I *do* need to confront him, and to let him know that I refuse to be bullied by him any longer. God knows I spent enough miserable years being bullied by his son! The thing that worries me is that he'll bring the whole weight of the judicial system down on my head until he gets the outcome that he wants—and that's Charlie.' She laid her hand over her chest to calm her racing heart. 'If the case goes to court I can't afford a good defence lawyer, and trust me…it's going to take someone very special and clever to face the intimidating might of Sir Christopher Abingdon.'

'Christopher Abingdon?' Jarrett's blue eyes visibly widened. '*He* was your father-in-law?'

'You know him?'

He shook his head, grimacing. 'I don't know him, but I know *of* him. I've seen him on enough political talk shows to know that he's perfectly odious and reprehensible. Don't worry about affording legal fees, my angel. I happen to have a very good friend in the legal realm—a man who is particularly dedicated to stamping out injustice wherever he finds it. If he can't represent you then he'll know someone who will. We'll find you the best damn lawyer money can buy, and that's a promise. Just don't tell me that you won't accept my help. It would mean a lot to me if you let me.'

As she absorbed the passionate intent of his words she relaxed against him in the realisation that, for the first time since she'd lost her father, she felt safe and secure in the presence of a man—a man she was slowly but surely beginning to allow herself to trust. To have Jarrett's sincere regard made Sophia feel more valued than she'd felt in a long, long time. It also lifted her spirits to know that at last someone really wanted to help her.

Raising her head, she knew her smile was a little shy, but she couldn't hide how much his words had meant to her. Before she could say a word Jarrett's hand had moved round to the back of her head to bring her face closer to his. *Then his mouth covered hers.* She had already had an example of how his kiss could make her dissolve, but *this* kiss—gently coaxing at first, then inexorably gathering in heat—was so gloriously seductive that she wondered how on earth she'd lived without his touch for so long.

The sultry caress quickly turned into a helpless, hungry demand that she couldn't help but rise to. As Jarrett's tongue melded hotly with hers and the roughened prickle of the beard that studded his jaw scratched against her skin his sensual ministrations sent her spinning. Suddenly she was caught in the eye of a storm that she didn't want to escape from.

When he cupped her breast through the thin jersey of her dress and teased the already rigid nipple between finger and thumb the force of the pleasurable groan that eased huskily from her throat didn't sound like the repressed and lonely woman of her hard, embittered marriage. *It didn't sound like her at all...* And when he carefully but firmly moved her off his lap to lay her on her back next to him she had not one single thought in her head about protesting. On the contrary, she just about contained herself from ripping his jacket and shirt from off his back so keen was her desire and need for him to love her.

As if reading her mind, he kicked off his shoes, then shrugged off his jacket. In less than a heartbeat he was leaning over her, his mouth continuing its exciting barrage on her senses, mind and body with luxuriously hot and exploring kisses to die for. But then came the dizzying point when even the most combustible kisses weren't enough…

'If you want me to stop then you have to tell me now, sweetheart. Although I'm strong I'm only human—and you're driving me wild.' Lifting his head, Jarrett threaded his fingers through Sophia's hair, smiling wryly down into her eyes.

'I don't want you to stop.' Her reply was a broken whisper of long-suppressed need and remembered heartache, but she knew there was no way on God's good green earth that she wanted to put an end to what they both so urgently desired.

'That's what I'd hoped you'd say,' Jarrett murmured, already reaching towards her to help her remove her dress.

In the flickering firelight as she lay down again, shivering in anticipation of what was to come, she was treated to a candid view of his fit male body as he disposed of his shirt. There was not one ounce of spare flesh on his hard-muscled chest with its smattering of ebony hair. And his strong arms with their silky, toned biceps were in a mouth-watering category all of their own. But her appreciative musings were instantly laid aside when he hungrily claimed her lips yet again and ran his hands lightly but expertly down over her body.

'You're so beautiful,' he murmured, his riveting blue eyes glancing passionately down into her face.

'So are you,' she answered.

'Does that mean that you now find me more appealing than when we first met?'

'I'm not going to encourage your vanity by saying anything further.'

'Good. Because I think the time for talking is past…at least for now. Don't you?'

He bent his head and put his lips to her breast. A spike of molten heat shot through her, rendering her boneless and making her tremble. The sensation was so off the scale of any barometer of pleasure she could have imagined that Sophia's eyelids drifted closed in order to deepen the deliciousness of the experience…to lose herself in a sensual world that for so long had been denied her. The moan that left her throat was soft and low, and as Jarrett's warm lips and beard-roughed jaw moved down over her heated skin, she drove her fingers through his silky cap of ebony hair.

For a moment she went rigid when his mouth dipped lower to caress the more sensitive skin between her thighs. After his long, lazily exploring kisses, the urgency that was building inside her was at breaking point, and suddenly she couldn't wait to hold him close and feel his body moving over hers, skin to skin…

'Jarrett…' His name left her lips on a breathy sigh, and he immediately responded by lifting his head and giving her a heart-stopping smile.

'What is it, sweetheart? Tell me what you need.'

Utterly transfixed by his devastating blue-eyed stare in the firelight, for a moment Sophia couldn't think straight. *Tell me what you need*… To answer the sexily-voiced command was almost beyond her powers, so alien was the sensual request.

'I need—I need you to love me,' she breathed.

In just a couple of effortlessly fluid movements Jarrett moved up, sat back and tugged off his jeans. Before he let them fall onto the floor he extricated his wallet and a small foil packet therein.

Her cheeks burned red at the impressive sight of his aroused sex, and in her mind she immediately scolded herself. *For goodness' sake, Sophia...it's not as though you're some untried virgin!* But the thought gave her no comfort, because it made her remember that she'd given her virginity to a man who had despised her.

As if intuiting that just such a thought had stolen into her mind, her would-be lover sheathed himself with his protection and carefully straddled her, stroking back her hair as he gazed deep into her eyes. 'Don't let the past spoil this time we have together,' he urged. 'Because everything's going to be all right.'

'It is?'

Any further speech she might have been going

to utter was silenced by the warm pressure of his mouth against hers. As she lost herself in the spell of the intimate duelling of their lips and tongues his hand deftly moved to the apex of her thighs to prise them apart, and in one smooth, urgent stroke he drove himself into her.

His possession was dizzying. More than that if felt so *right*. Tears surged hotly into Sophia's eyes. When Jarrett started to move rhythmically inside her she wound her arms round his neck to invite even more of his incendiary kisses, but he glanced down at her with surprised concern when he saw the moisture that slid down her face.

'What's wrong? Am I hurting you?'

'Nothing's wrong. Everything's *perfect*, in fact…promise.'

'But—'

Now it was *her* turn to silence him with a lingering and sexy open-mouthed kiss. She sensed his pleasure straight away, because he began to move inside her with more purpose and intent, anchoring his hands round her hips and urging her to wrap her thighs round him as he rocked into her more deeply. Catching her breath, Sophia dug her nails into his back and held him to her with all her strength. Suddenly the powerful waves of pleasure that were transporting her to only one destination crested, and the resultant erotic laps of blissful heat that throbbed through her entire being made her gasp out loud.

The lovely emerald eyes that glanced up at him had never appeared more beautiful, Jarrett thought, even though it was the heart-rending glitter of tears that rendered them especially bewitching tonight. But all further thought was suspended as he sensed her muscles clasp him hotly and contract. Clasping her arms about his neck even more tightly, she murmured his name with what sounded very much like a sob.

Dear God! He could lose himself in this woman's charms for ever and not regret a single moment he spent with her whether he lived to be a hundred or died tomorrow. No other woman had made him feel this good, this glad to be a man...*ever.*

As his lover's breathy little gasps died away he

could no longer keep a grip on the wild storm of need that held him in thrall, and as his desire peaked and soared beyond the point of no return his body convulsed hard. The fierce shout that left his throat was inevitable. The only sound he heard straight after that was the creak of the old couch's springs as he lay down in his lover's arms. With her gentle fingers tunnelling in and out of his hair, Sophia's warmly velvet lips pressed tenderly against his cheek.

'Are you all right?' she enquired softly.

Jarrett raised his head to examine her with a mixture of amusement and disbelief. '"All right" doesn't even begin to describe how I feel. I'm ecstatic...in heaven. Can't you tell?'

Her cheeks dimpled with pleasure. 'My great-aunt Mary would be scandalised if she knew what we had just done on her antique couch.'

'Maybe she would...maybe she wouldn't.'

Her green eyes widened in surprise, 'Are you suggesting that Great-Aunt Mary *wasn't* the terribly proper, stiff-upper-lipped lady that she presented to the world?'

Grinning, Jarrett waggled his eyebrows. 'I haven't a clue what the lady was like, but don't forget appearances can be deceptive. Don't you think it might be nice to imagine that underneath her very proper exterior she yearned to let her hair down and have a little fun? You said she lived on her own. Was she ever married?'

Thinking back over the scant history her father had told her, Sophia lightly shook her head and sighed. 'No. She stayed single all her life. My dad once told me it was because she didn't particularly like men.'

'That doesn't mean she didn't have any lovers...does it?'

'I suppose it doesn't.' She reddened a little. 'Anyway...she's gone now, and if she found some pleasure in the arms of someone, good luck to her! She's been very good to me, leaving me this incredible old house, and I'll never forget her.'

The fire spat and hissed in the grate, and the robust log that Sophia had laid at its centre cracked and settled deeper into its fiery bed. Gazing down into her flushed beautiful face,

Jarrett moved, tugging the prettily patterned eiderdown over them both. Lying down again, he arranged a cushion behind his head, then put his arm protectively round her slender shoulders. As she willingly rested her head on his chest her silky hair felt like the softest down against his skin, and, his body throbbing warmly in the aftermath of their lovemaking, he marvelled at the sense of perfect rightness that rolled over him.

There was no doubt in his mind that being with Sophia was the best thing that had ever happened to him. And now that he'd made love to her Jarrett made a silent vow that if it was at all in his power he would never let any danger threaten her again. The gentle glow of the firelight and the lamp on the small mahogany side table hadn't been able to hide the fading scars he'd glimpsed here and there on her supple, slender body, and he'd had to tamp down the anger that had threatened to choke him at the sight. Men who hit women were the lowest of the low in his book.

A sense of urgency gripped him to help her deal with the despicable father-in-law who was still intimidating her and get him out of her hair for good. What he and her worthless husband had put her through was nothing less than criminal, and the remaining perpetrator shouldn't get off scot-free. *Not if Jarrett had anything to do with it.*

As Sophia settled herself more comfortably against him, she covered her mouth to suppress a yawn. 'I'm sorry,' she apologized. 'I guess my broken night's sleep has caught up with me.'

'There's no need to apologise. Why don't you just let yourself drift off? I'll stay here with you until the morning.'

'Will you really? It's not exactly the most comfortable couch in the world to sleep on.'

'I give you my word. Now try and get some sleep.'

Sophia was still sleeping when Jarrett peered out between the closed red velvet drapes at the window and saw that it was daylight. The fire in the grate had long gone out, and the temperature in the lofty room was icy enough to make him wince.

Making his way back to the couch, he carefully arranged the quilt more snugly round Sophia's pale shoulders. She stirred a little, but didn't wake. In repose, her lovely face looked peaceful and young. A faint smile raised the corners of his mouth. Rubbing his hands to warm them, he turned on his heel and moved across to the fireplace to rebuild the fire. He didn't want Sophia waking up to a cold room. After that he made his way to the kitchen.

Ten minutes later, sitting at the old-fashioned breakfast table with its dented and scratched oak surface, revived by a steaming mug of strong black coffee, he searched for his lawyer friend's phone number on his mobile and rang him. He knew for a fact he would already be at his desk. After a long, heated conversation he ended the call and got restlessly to his feet. He hadn't mentioned Christopher Abingdon's name, but it had been enough for him to tell his friend that Sophia's father-in-law was a renowned QC for him to get the bit between his teeth and promise to do all he could to help just as soon as Sophia personally instructed him to act on her behalf. The case was 'potential dynamite', he said.

Staring out of the window at the shadowy back garden, where a large portion of the light was cut off by the untamed shrubs growing wild, he was deep in thought when—still attired in the pretty blue dress of the night before and with her hair endearingly tousled—the lady herself appeared at the kitchen door tiredly rubbing her eyes.

'Good morning.'

'Morning, sleepyhead.'

'You made up the fire in the living room. Thanks for that.'

'The temperature put me in mind of Siberia when I woke up, and I didn't want you to be cold. Want some coffee? I hope you don't mind, but I made a pot.'

'Of course I don't mind.' Her smile was a little uncertain, almost as if she didn't quite know how to proceed after the passion that had erupted between them last night. After tucking some hair behind her ear, she crossed her arms over her chest as if to warm herself. 'I thought you might have had to dash off. I didn't mean to lie in so long. I'm normally up at the crack of dawn, and I'm a light sleeper. If I hear so much as a sparrow cough it wakes me up.'

Jarrett chuckled. 'I've no intention of dashing off—if that's okay with you? It's not even eight in the morning—surely you're entitled to have the odd lie-in? Especially when Charlie's staying at his uncle's.' In truth, he had plenty of work to get on with at home, but he'd already decided that it wouldn't take priority over being with Sophia today.

'I'd really like it if you stayed for a while. But I'll say no to your offer of coffee, thanks. What I'm most in need of right now is a shower and a change of clothing. No doubt you feel the same?'

'Are you suggesting that we take a shower together?' Keeping his tone teasingly light, he moved to stand in front of her. At first Sophia seemed to find it inordinately difficult to meet his glance. But then Jarrett lifted her hand and raised it slowly to his lips, leaving the warm imprint of his mouth against her fingers. His senses were already rioting at her touch and her sweetly addictive scent.

His romantic gesture brought the smile to her face that he'd hoped for. 'Maybe…maybe we could do that some other time? Right now I'd just really like to freshen up. You're welcome to jump in after me, though.'

'Fair enough…but you don't know what you're missing.' He grinned.

Sophia's emerald eyes visibly darkened. 'That's not true after last night. I don't think I'll ever forget what you did for me, Jarrett.'

'What I did *for* you?' He was puzzled.

'I mean the way you turned up in the middle of the night like that…just when I needed you.'

He suddenly realised that he was still holding her hand. He used it to impel her firmly into his arms. 'Don't you know that I needed you too, Sophia?'

The last thing he registered just before he kissed her was the gentle quiver of her lips as he lowered his head and helplessly and hungrily crushed his mouth to hers…

CHAPTER NINE

JARRETT had showered, and apart from knowing that Sophia had used the cramped cubicle before him it had not been the most salubrious experience of his life. Clearly her great-aunt had not considered a little luxury in the bathroom high on her list of priorities, and the addition of a shower stall in the Victorian bathroom looked to have been installed somewhat grudgingly.

At any rate, it had forced him to be somewhat creative with his use of the slow trickle of barely warm water that emanated from the shower head. It had taken a long time to rinse Sophia's vanilla and honey scented shampoo from his hair, so he'd simply spent the extra time recalling every sensually intimate detail of their lovemaking the night before. Maybe he should have tried harder to persuade her that they ought to shower together?

Abruptly turning off the water, he stepped out of the cubicle. Brusquely drying himself with the generous-sized white bathtowel that had been thoughtfully left folded neatly over the back of a rattan chair for his use, he scowled when he realised there was no radiator to warm it.

Other than dwelling on his sexual frustration, and the fact that the temperature in the room was cold enough to give him hypothermia, he forced himself to think about topics less apt to make him irritable.

Examining the room, he observed the tired furnishings and fittings that predominated. The space was generous and high-ceilinged, with beautifully moulded carved cornices, but in Jarrett's opinion it cried out for the decor and fittings that would enhance the property's stately appeal. It made him eager to call an interior designer friend of his and arrange for his company to fit a completely new bathroom for Sophia and her son. One that would have all the modern day accoutrements and luxury anyone could desire but would be sensitively done to enhance the grandeur and history of this beautiful old house.

One step at a time, he told himself. Even though he genuinely had her wellbeing at heart, he had to be careful not to make assumptions about her needs.

Dressed again in the jeans and black sweatshirt he'd worn on his three a.m. dash to the house, he returned downstairs to the kitchen, quietly whistling some bars of Puccini. There was no sign of the lady of the house. Curious as to where she might be, because after her shower he'd left her in the drawing room combing out her long damp hair in front of the fire, Jarrett proceeded along the corridor outside the kitchen, knocking on doors, calling out her name and opening them if there wasn't a reply.

Right at the back of the house he heard sounds that suggested furniture being moved or rearranged. He approached the wide open door he'd seen, and came to a standstill in the doorway at the surprising sight that met his eyes. Sophia appeared to be vainly trying to shift a tall metal cabinet on her own, and the task was obviously getting the better of her. She'd tied back her newly dried chestnut hair into some kind of loose top-knot, and was clearly hot and a little bothered from her physical exertions. She impatiently blew some gently drifting strands of hair out of her eyes and cursed softly.

The picture she made was utterly endearing… sexy too. Dressed in the faded blue jeans with the ragged hole in the knee, and an old green and white checked shirt that might have been a man's, she could easily have graced any men's 'lifestyle' magazine with her arresting image.

Charmed and amused, and not a little turned-on all at the same time, Jarrett folded his arms and grinned. 'What are you doing, wrestling with that metallic monster? Moving it or beating it into submission?'

The emerald-green eyes in front of him flashed with enough electricity to start a fire. 'Very funny… Instead of making fun of me you *could* give me a hand, you know!'

'I wasn't making fun of you.' His mood immediately sobered. 'Where do you want this archaic monstrosity moved to?'

'I want to move it out into the corridor for the time being.'

'Let's do it, then.'

'I'm sorry. I'm apt to be a little tetchy in the mornings.'

'No need for an apology. What are you intending to do in here?'

'Remember I told you that I was going to create a darkroom for my photography? Well, this is going to be it. It will be such a boon to have my own instead of paying a photographic company to print my photographs for me. Once upon a time this must have been some kind of utility room, but I think my aunt must have used it as a repository for junk mostly. The great thing is it's got an old ceramic sink in it with running water, which can be my wet area for processing. But first of all I have to move all the old furniture out and clean the place up. Then I want to scrub down the walls and paint them white.'

'That's a new one on me...white for a dark-room?'

'That's right.'

Sophia dropped her hands from round the metal cabinet as Jarrett took over and carefully stood it upright again. He paused to hear what she had to say next before he transferred the furniture out into the corridor, catching the faint tantalising drift of her perfume as he did so.

'I've learned that white is the best colour for a darkroom. It helps save time trying to block out light spills.'

'Well...if you need a hand with the painting... or anything else for that matter...I'm your man.'

'Are you indeed?'

Sophia took the wind out of his sails with a teasing little smile that all but cut him off at the knees. If she thought he could stay immune to such a provocative gesture then Jarrett was sorry—but he was only human. It was tanta-mount to expecting bees to keep away from a dripping honeypot.

Brushing the dust from the cabinet off his

hands, he caught her by the waist and impelled her firmly into his arms. The heat in him was already on simmer even before he held her. 'If I'm not already...then I want you to know that I fully intend to be.'

'You're very sure of yourself!'

'I told you before. When it comes to the things that are important to me I state what I want and go for it. It's always been a policy of mine to err on the side of confidence.'

'Well...if you're feeling so confident perhaps you'd like to cook us some breakfast? I don't know about you, but I'm starving. I have to confess that any kind of physical work never fails to stimulate my appetite.' Her lips shaped another saucily provocative grin.

Before he answered Jarrett paid her back by delivering a slow, no-holds-barred sexy kiss on her open mouth, drowning in her sweetly honeyed flavours. His passionate siege made her go limp in his arms. Satisfied he'd got the response he wanted, he made a Herculean effort to manfully resist further arousing temptation and smiled lazily down into her stunned green eyes instead.

'I'll happily cook us breakfast—but only if you promise to stay with me in the kitchen and keep me company. That way at least I can look at you from time to time. Then, after we've eaten, I'll make a start helping you with the darkroom.'

'Are you usually so amenable when a girlfriend asks you to do something?'

His hands moved from either side of her slim waist down to the trim, shapely hips encased in softly napped denim and he held them fast, rocking her even closer into his body. The intimate contact almost made him groan out loud. It was still a thrill to him that Sophia allowed him such liberties—especially when her trust in men could very easily have been rendered obsolete by her deceased husband's cruel exploits.

'So you're my girlfriend now, are you?' He almost held his breath as he waited for her reply, even though he'd kept his tone teasingly light.

In answer, Sophia endeavoured to give a nonchalant shrug, but the sparkle in her eyes betrayed her. 'I suppose I must be…since we've slept together. I'm old-fashioned like that, I'm afraid. I've never seen sex as a form of recreation. I don't think it should ever be taken lightly.'

'Well…' Bending his head, Jarrett lifted her hair to place a provocative kiss on the enticing juncture between her shoulder and neck. The combination of her silkily warm skin and her body's naturally sexy scent instantly hardened him. 'It's lucky that I have a penchant for old-fashioned girls like you, isn't it?'

Jarrett wasn't the only one finding it hard to resist temptation. A small gasp of breathily-voiced pleasure escaped Sophia's lips. 'Didn't you—didn't you say that you were working from home today?' she asked, a small frown puckering her brow.

As she met his smiling gaze her pretty face was rosily flushed, and the tantalising rise and fall of her chest beneath the checked shirt she wore illustrated that she was nowhere near as calm and unaffected as she might be endeavouring to portray.

'I did. But if the choice is between working and being with you then I'm afraid there's no contest. I'd much rather spend the day here, being your odd job man, than trying to get my head around work…that is if you have no objection?'

'That's…that's fine with me.'

'Good. So the first thing on the agenda is cooking breakfast, is it? I mean, you wouldn't like to take a little R&R first?' His fingers were busy slipping the buttons of her shirt through their buttonholes even as he talked.

'As lovely as that sounds—*ahh*—how am I supposed to even think straight when you—when you—?' Her even white teeth clamped heavily down on her plump lower lip as Jarrett slipped the final three buttons free from their buttonholes and, curling his fingers round the two cotton sides of her shirt, opened them to reveal the prettily embroidered white bra she wore underneath. 'You don't play fair.'

Her hand clamped onto his wrist to halt his eager aim to slip her shirt off of her shoulders, and with satisfaction he sensed it tremble.

'But playing is exactly what I have in mind before I cook you the best breakfast you'll ever eat,' he told her, meaningfully lowering his voice.

'I'd love to, but—'

'I don't like the sound of *but*…'

'Jarrett…I've honestly got to crack on with this darkroom. It's important for my livelihood. Please try and understand.'

A second or two passed as he strove to get his amorous mood in check. Then he started to refasten the buttons on the shirt that he'd hoped would be just the *first* item of her clothing that he removed. 'I do understand—but can I help it if you're just too damn tempting for words?'

'That lascivious look could tempt a nun from her vows, and I'm sure you know it, but luckily for me I have a will of iron,' Sophia quipped back.

'Lucky, is it? Forgive me if I can't agree. Oh, well… I suppose I'd better try and distract myself by cooking that breakfast. At least it will keep me out of mischief for a while. But I can't promise that I won't try to get you naked later.'

When he started to move away, with a rueful smile playing about his lips, Sophia laid her hand on his arm, her expression suddenly serious. 'Jarrett? It's not that I don't want to make love with you again, because I do. Last night was—well, it was incredible. You made me feel like a woman again, instead of just an empty husk of the girl I used to be. It's just that while Charlie is away this is too good an opportunity to make some real progress with my darkroom.'

'You're right. Of course it is. With my help you can get a fair amount done, too.'

'Thanks.' She smoothed back some drifting stray hairs that had escaped from her loosely fashioned topknot and the smile she gifted him with was intimately warm. 'I also wanted to say thank you again for coming to my rescue in the middle of the night, and for agreeing to stay here with me today.'

'It's me who should be thanking *you*.' Jarrett's response was instantaneous and heartfelt. He deplored the idea that she might have even momentarily doubted he would want to stay. Catching her hand, he turned it over in his palm, then lifted it towards him to gently touch his mouth to her softly folded fingers. 'And I'm here because I want to be, Sophia. I'd rather be here with you than anywhere else. Now, I suppose I'd better let you lead me to the kitchen before you accuse me of trying to starve you into submission.'

'I would never try to coerce you into anything you didn't want to do...by fair means or foul. If you think I would then you really need to get to know me better.' Finishing her comment with a grin, and with her hand still in his, she spun round to pull him firmly towards the door. 'But I have to tell you I'm highly intrigued to know whether you can cook half as well as you kiss, Mr Gaskill, and I'm warning you...you'd better not disappoint me!'

Jarrett had indeed cooked Sophia the best breakfast she'd ever eaten. She shouldn't have been at all surprised, because it seemed that the man could undertake any task given him and make it look like a master-class in effortless ease. And when they'd both moved back to her great-aunt's old junk room to start work on transforming it into the darkroom she craved they'd worked alongside each other in complete harmony—moving furniture out into the hallway, briskly sweeping the stone-flagged floor clean after every item was removed.

As if by unspoken consent they kept their conversation light, with a fair amount of mutual banter. But it wasn't long before Sophia became aware that they were both trying hard to resist the powerful undercurrent of electricity that sparked between them whenever their gazes inadvertently met and held. *She felt like an excited bride-to-be on the eve of her wedding day.* And it wasn't just Jarrett's compelling dark looks or his tender lovemaking that fuelled her growing attraction towards him. His unfailing good humour was a powerful incentive too. Although sometimes she found herself holding her breath, in case his light-hearted teasing turned into a cruel or unkind barb, it never did.

It bitterly saddened her to realise yet again that

the desolate and painful years with her husband had set up a belief in her to *expect* to be treated badly by a man. Was she really going to let that soul-destroying experience dictate the pattern of the rest of her days? What effect might such a way of being have on Charlie? *It hardly bore contemplation.* No. If she wanted to change such a damaging belief then she had to be more determined to learn to trust…to anticipate love and respect instead of the hatred, mockery and deceit she'd lived with for far too long.

'Jarrett?'

'Hmm?' He was halfway across the room, moving the last item of unwanted furniture—a squat gate-legged table—out into the corridor. He set it down on the stone flags and dusted off his hands.

To Sophia's amusement she saw that he had acquired a fair amount of dust on his sculpted cheekbones, as well as in his curling ebony hair. Crossing over to him she reached up on tiptoe to plant an affectionate kiss on his mouth.

'What's that for?' The timbre of his voice was a little husky and his gaze became more intense.

'You indicated when we first met that you were rather partial to apple pie.'

'I did?'

'Yes, you did. You came up to me at the market, remember? You asked me if I wanted an extra guest for tea.'

'So I did.' His hands settled lightly either side of her hips as his beautifully carved lips quirked a smile. 'My mother always taught me that if you don't ask you don't get.'

'I thought I'd nip out to the corner shop and buy some cooking apples to make you one…as a reward for all your help. Sound good?'

'Sounds very good…except for the fact that I don't want you to go.'

'I'll only be gone about twenty minutes.'

'Trust me—it will feel like a lifetime.'

Dipping his head towards her, Jarrett delivered a melting kiss that buckled Sophia's knees the instant his lips touched hers. As his tongue dived hotly into her mouth, eliciting a helpless moan from her, it made her think about the exciting possibility of whiling away the rest of the afternoon in bed with him. The thought made her tremble. Funny how the imperative to get on with her darkroom suddenly waned in light of such a provocative alternative...

Consequently it took every ounce of will-power to extricate herself from his enticing embrace so that she could carry out her mission to bake him an apple pie. 'I won't be long,' she said, and with her heart racing she smiled cheerfully and headed for the door. 'I promise.'

Rowena Phillips—the middle-aged brunette with the rather severely pencilled-in eyebrows who ran the local corner shop—had never exhibited the least bit of friendliness towards Sophia before. In fact there were times when she'd been downright unhelpful—hostile, even. As far as Sophia knew, all she'd done to warrant such an attitude was to arrive in the village as a stranger and keep herself to herself. But now, as the door swung shut behind her with the tinkle of a melodic bell to announce her entrance, the older woman's small dark eyes widened with peculiar interest as she recognised her customer.

'Hello, dear. What can I do for you today?'

Her voice had acquired the kind of fake cheeriness that immediately put Sophia on her guard. Her glance honed in on the basket of cooking apples in the aisle opposite the newspapers, and she helped herself to one of the brown paper bags that hung suspended from a small nail above. 'I'd just like three or four cooking apples, thanks,' she answered distractedly, wanting to pay for the fruit and get out of there as quickly as possible.

'Baking an apple pie, are we?'

'Yes, I am, as a matter of fact.'

Flustered by the unwanted attention, Sophia quickly slipped three large green apples into a paper bag and approached the counter. As the woman relieved her of the bag to weigh them on the scales, Sophia saw that she was deliberately taking her time about it. It quickly became obvious that she had something on her mind that she wanted to share.

'I see that you've become very friendly with

our local landowner, Mr Gaskill,' she remarked. 'Wasn't that his Range Rover that I saw parked outside High Ridge this morning?'

For a dizzying moment Sophia was dumb-struck. Feeling her cheeks flush hotly in embar-rassment, she agitatedly closed the purse she'd just taken from her jacket pocket and opened in readiness to pay for the apples. 'What possible business is it of yours or anyone else's who I'm friendly with?' she answered through numbed lips, suddenly wishing that she'd ignored the spontaneous urge to bake Jarrett an apple pie and stayed home with him instead.

'I was only being neighbourly, Ms Markham… But you keep yourself to yourself, don't you? A small village like this…well, we're apt to notice things like that.'

'That I value my privacy, you mean?'

'No. That one of our most successful local busi-nessmen is parked outside your house in the early hours of the morning.'

'I'd like to pay for the apples, if you don't mind. I'm in a hurry.'

In response Rowena Phillips curtly stated the price, holding out her hand at the same time. Sophia opened her purse and counted out the right money. Lifting up the bag of apples, she dropped them into her hessian shopping bag. Intent on leaving, she was about to turn away when the shop's presumptuous proprietor added another barbed aside.

'You *do* know that Jarrett Gaskill has always wanted to own High Ridge Hall, don't you? I heard he made several attempts to try and buy it when Miss Wingham died, but you obviously pipped him to the post.'

Inside her chest Sophia's heart was thundering so hard that she suddenly felt quite faint. She struggled to make the words teeming in her brain leave her lips. 'Exactly what are you trying to say, Mrs Phillips?'

The woman folded her fleshy arms across her turtleneck sweater. 'All I'm saying is that perhaps you should be wary of getting to know him, Ms Markham. A wealthy property developer might use any means possible to get the property or land that he wants…don't you think?'

'What I think is that you really should keep your nose out of other people's business.'

As she walked back down the country road to where she'd parked her car several distressing thoughts ran through Sophia's mind all at once. Jarrett had already told her that he was a rich *landowner*—but he'd said nothing about buying property, too. To learn of his interest in High Ridge had come as a great shock. The obnoxious shopkeeper had said he'd made several attempts to purchase it. Why had he never told her? Surely it was obvious that she'd be interested?

She felt sick to her stomach. She'd been utterly foolish to trust him. If only she'd stuck to her initial suspicions when they first met that it was the house that drew him and not her! What was she going to do now? As well as entrusting him with the distressing and painful details of her doomed marriage she'd also made love with him…and that had been no insignificant thing.

Because during their short association she'd lost her heart to the man. *Dear God.*

She murmured ,as she turned the key in the car door with a hand that wouldn't stop shaking, and by the time she'd arrived back at the house and walked up to her front door she was so angry and fearful that she'd been duped that she left the shopping bag with the apples in on the back seat of the car along with her intention to bake a pie.

As soon as she turned her key in the lock the door was wrenched eagerly open from the inside and a smiling Jarrett—dust still evident in his curling dark hair and on his cheek—appeared in front of her. Before he uttered a single word, she passionately burst out, 'Why didn't you tell me that you'd tried to buy High Ridge?'

The words came out on a broken sob as she blindly pushed past him into the hallway.

CHAPTER TEN

'WHO have you been talking to?' Scraping his hand through his hair in bewilderment, Jarrett spun round on his heel and tore down the corridor. He caught up with Sophia just as she stepped through the drawing room door. His heart threatened to burst out of his chest as he grabbed her arm to halt her flight. 'Who told you that I wanted to buy High Ridge? I wasn't trying to keep it a secret from you, but I'd like to know who told you.'

Her expression was more distressed than he'd ever seen it.

'So it's true, then? In that case does it matter who told me?' Shaking her arm free from his hold, she stared up at him with emerald eyes that shimmered with tears. 'What I want to know is, are you here because you really like me, Jarrett, or is it merely because you hope that I'll sell High

Ridge to you? I hear you made several attempts to try and buy it before I arrived. Is that also true?'

Telling himself to remain calm, and not let some interfering busybody's spin on his intentions cloud his reason, Jarrett dropped his hands to his hips and shook his head. 'I wanted to buy this place when I heard the owner had died. As someone who's always admired beautiful architecture, I had a yen to restore it to its former glory and perhaps one day live in it myself. But buying it ceased to be important after I met you, Sophia. If you honestly think I'd be so conniving that I would *pretend* to be attracted to you for the sole purpose of getting the chance to purchase your house, then I'm pretty devastated. If you'd rather believe some stranger's incriminating story about me than my own testimony I honestly don't know how we can regain the trust that I thought we were building. I know you've been badly hurt in the past, but I'm not a liar or a cheat or a bully. The last thing—the *very* last thing I would ever do is use you or abuse you. I'm shaken to my core to think for even a second that you could believe that I would.'

'But why didn't you tell me that you'd been interested in the house?'

'What was the point? It's *your* house…you inherited it from your family. If I was so intent on persuading you to sell it to me then why would I offer to make you a loan to help you keep it?'

Sophia hung her head for a moment, clearly busy processing what he'd said. When she raised it again to study him, he could see by her quivering lip and desolate gaze that she was even more distraught than before.

'You're right…it doesn't make sense. But I reacted the way I did because it was my worst fear, you see…that you only wanted the house and not—and not me.'

Although Jarrett ached with every fibre of his being to take her in his arms, to hold her tight and reassure her, he didn't. The idea came into his head that perhaps he had pushed too hard too soon to persuade her to enter into a relationship with him. Seeing how shaken she was

after listening to some gossip put damning be-
liefs about him in her head, he suddenly knew
that he needed to back off a little and give her
some space. Given time, would she come round
to realising that he honestly *did* have her best in-
terests at heart and would never deceive her? *He
really hoped so.* He had felt sick to his stomach
when she'd looked at him so accusingly just now.
After spending that one incredible night with her
in his arms he already knew that he would never
want any other woman but *her*. But it was clear
that the bird with a broken wing he'd likened her
to still needed more time to heal.

'You should stop scaring yourself. Try to realise instead how much you have to offer any
man, Sophia. You should also believe and trust
in your ability to discern truth from lies. Does
your heart tell you that I've been deceiving you?'
he asked.

She shook her head, her hand rubbing away
the moisture that glistened on her cheek. 'No, it
doesn't. When I heard that I'm afraid I just panicked. Fear has had such a hold on me for so long

that I've fallen into the habit of waiting for the other shoe to drop…for something to go wrong. I always think that if something good happens then I'll have to pay for it in some way. It's like I don't deserve it. That's all I can say in my defence, Jarrett. I'm so sorry that I was angry with you. I truly regret it.'

This time Jarrett *did* pull Sophia into his arms. As he enfolded her she shuddered and laid her head against his chest. Lifting his hand, he gently stroked his fingers up and down the back of her velvety-soft neck. 'You blame yourself too much,'

'You're probably right about that. I promise I'll try to change and be less unkind to myself…more optimistic.'

'That would be good. But don't change too much.' He slid his fingers beneath her chin so that he could gaze down into her long-lashed emerald eyes. 'There's nothing wrong with the way you are. You react the way you do sometimes because you've been hurt. It's perfectly understandable. In light of that, it makes sense that you need to give yourself some proper time to heal, to regain your self-confidence.'

With a thoughtful sigh, Jarrett drew the pad of his thumb down over her damp cheek. 'That's why I want to honour that need. You're still the only woman I want to be with, Sophia, but if our relationship is going to have a chance at all then you need time to work things out for yourself. To reach your own decisions about things without my influence. What I'm leading up to is that I suggest we have a break from seeing each other for a while.'

The shock that registered in her eyes tore at his heart, but Jarrett steeled himself against changing his mind. He was convinced this was the right thing to do. To act in any other way would be to put his own wants and needs before hers, and he'd already vowed not to do that. That was what her brutish husband had done, and he'd seen for himself the damaging effects.

Slowly but surely Sophia extricated herself from his arms. When she was satisfied that there was enough space between them, she folded her arms tightly over her chest. Her lips quivered. 'All right, then. I agree. I see where you're coming from. I didn't trust you—I'm not surprised you want a break. Maybe even a permanent one.'

'I don't want a permanent break. I'm genuinely thinking of *you*, Sophia. And while we're apart if you need me for anything—anything at all— I'm there for you. I give you my word on that.'

'Thanks.' She shrugged. Her discomfort was painful to witness.

'I mean what I say. There's just one other thing I wanted to mention.'

'What's that?'

Hearing the slight catch in her voice, Jarrett had to steel himself for a second time not to take back his suggestion. Reaching into the back pocket of his jeans, he took out a small notebook and pencil and wrote down a number, which he handed to Sophia. 'This is the number of a lawyer friend of mine. I've already spoken to him and outlined the problem you've been having with your ex father-in-law. Needless to say I've mentioned no names, but my friend was instantly interested in helping you. He's a good man, and if anyone can bring about an end to this intimidation he can. I want you to give him a ring, and I want you to do it soon. You've lived with the threat of losing Charlie for far too long.'

Examining the slip of lined paper Jarrett gave her, Sophia thought it was a wonder she could make out a letter or digit through the hot blur of tears that clouded her gaze. *Jarrett was breaking off their liaison and it was all her fault.* She'd elected to believe some stupid comments she'd heard from a mean-spirited gossip over the kindness and generosity of a man who really cared for her. How could she have been so short-sighted and stupid?

She folded the note and slipped it into the pocket on the front of her shirt. 'I promise I'll ring,' she murmured.

'Sophia?'

'Yes?'

'Don't put off ringing him because you're worried about how much a consultation will cost. I've already arranged with my friend for him to send the bill to me. And if it transpires that you decide to sue Abingdon for damages then I'll foot the bill for that, too.'

Swallowing hard, Sophia made herself bring her glance level with Jarrett's. His blue eyes glittered like incandescent sunlight over a still lake, and she could swear she heard her heart crack. 'One day I'll pay you back for all the kindness you've shown me…that's my promise to you, Jarrett.'

'You owe me nothing.' His voice was slightly gruff, as though he was struggling with emotion.

'Let me be the judge of that, will you?' She offered him the most tenderly loving smile that she could manage. It was a poor reflection of the torrent of love and longing that poured so helplessly into her heart.

Three days after she'd tearfully said goodbye to Jarrett, Sophia found herself on a train to London. She'd taken his advice and had an appointment with his lawyer friend. Now she was intent on facing one of her worst fears—holding her ex father-in-law to account not just for his own vile intimidation of her, but his son's too.

She'd done a lot of thinking since Jarrett had suggested they take a break, and their being apart had made her realise that she didn't want the themes of regret and loss to be the pervading story of her life. Nor did she want anyone else to have power over her. So, instead of running away and hoping for the best, she would face her fears head-on instead. She refused to spend one more night in fear that Christopher Abingdon might exploit some loophole in the law to take Charlie away from her.

The buildings that housed the elite coterie of lawyers in Lincoln's Inn were grand and imposing, with a long and distinguished history, but as Sophia mounted the stone steps of one of the grandest buildings in the tranquil urban enclave she refused to be intimidated. And if she wavered for an instant all she had to do was think of her son and how he deserved a mother who was courageous, who would do anything to ensure his wellbeing now and in the future, no matter what the cost to herself.

In the opulent waiting room, with its stately antique furniture and solemn portraits of imperious-looking lawyers of bygone days, she flicked through a copy of *Tatler* magazine to while away the time. But she barely registered the glossy contents because the adrenaline pumping through her body made her impervious to anything but the all-important and possibly life-changing interview that lay ahead of her.

When Jarrett had endured his first self-inflicted separation from Sophia—after he'd wrongly mistaken her brother for her lover—he had been sullen and ill-tempered with anyone who'd happened to rub him up the wrong way. And it hadn't taken much—just a glance that lingered a little too long had been enough to ignite his temper. That was until she'd confronted him with the truth. But their being apart this time had made him turn in on himself rather than inflict his bad temper or desolate mood on anyone else.

At first he chose to bury himself in his work, but when he wasn't distracting himself with that he returned to missing Sophia unbearably, and the interminable ache in his heart grew worse. Had Charlie returned from his visit to his uncle? If he had, Jarrett hoped that his presence might help ease the pain in her eyes that he'd witnessed when he'd suggested they spend some time apart for a while. Even now he wondered how he had been strong enough to make such a suggestion. It barely consoled him that he'd done it for her own good, so that she might take the proper time out to heal.

Today, three days into their separation, he'd received a dinner invitation—or rather a *command*—from his sister Beth. Unsure whether he could face another long evening on his own, with nothing for company but his increasingly desperate desire to see Sophia, he'd reluctantly elected to go. Besides, he told himself, they hadn't spoken since she'd rung to apologise for suggesting he was getting close to Sophia purely because he wanted High Ridge. It didn't sit right with him that they hadn't properly made up yet.

'Hello, stranger!'

Beth threw her arms round Jarrett in a waft of her favourite Dior perfume, and he couldn't help but hug her back. Tonight she looked relaxed and pretty in an uncharacteristically casual ensemble of pink sweatshirt and faded blue jeans. In contrast, he still wore the Armani suit he'd donned for a board meeting in London. Not wanting to appear as uptight as he felt inside, he reached up and loosened his navy silk tie.

'Dinner's about half an hour away,' she informed him cheerily. 'Why don't you come and join me in the kitchen and we can chat as I put the finishing touches to it?'

'Okay,' he agreed, wondering why all the house lights were off apart from in the hallway and kitchen. 'Where's Paul?'

Beth rolled her eyes. 'Gone to see his mother in Exeter. He'll be gone for a few days. I'll miss him, but I actually think it's good for couples to have some time apart. It makes the heart grow fonder, as the saying goes. Anyway, I thought it would be a good opportunity for us to catch up with what's been happening.'

'Hmm...' Suddenly wary, and knowing he'd have to take a view on how much or how little to share as the evening progressed, Jarrett stood the bottle of fine red wine he'd brought on the marbled surface of the kitchen counter. 'Shall I open this?'

'Yes, please.' His sister was suddenly at his side, examining the vintage of the bottle. 'Impeccable taste, as usual. Mind if we keep it simple and eat in here?' She nodded towards the white marble island where she had set two places.

'Good idea. I'm all for keeping things simple,' he murmured, unable to keep the irony entirely out of his tone.

'Well, you pour the wine and I'll get my ingredients together for custard to go with the apple crumble. We're having beef bourguignon for the main, and I thought I'd make your favourite dessert to go with it rather than anything fancy.'

'Thanks.' He opened the wine and left it to

breathe as he collected two slim-stemmed glasses from the cabinet on the other side of the room— all the while painfully remembering that Sophia never had made the apple pie she'd promised him. All because some poisonous gossipmonger had made her doubt his sincerity.

'Jarrett?' His sister was giving him one of her deeply penetrating looks that he knew prefigured an uncomfortable query into his private life.

Tensing, he kept his gaze focused on the two elegant wine glasses he'd set down side by side on the counter. 'Yes?'

'You seem a little subdued this evening. Is everything all right? I mean, there aren't any hard feelings about what I said at the party?'

'You mean about my reason for getting to know Sophia?'

'Yes. You are still friends with her, I take it?'

'Yes. We're still friends.'

The heavy sigh Beth released made Jarrett immediately lock his reluctant gaze with hers. 'I'm getting the distinct feeling you want to be more than just friends with her. Am I right?' she gently quizzed him. 'You *can* talk to me about it, you know. Contrary to what you might believe, I can be discreet.'

'I'd like to believe that—I really would—but having recently experienced the damaging effects of idle gossip I'm not in a hurry to share my thoughts or feelings with anyone...even *you*.' Suddenly restless, he waved his hand towards the bottle atop the marble counter. 'Shall I pour us a glass of wine?' he suggested.

'Sure.'

Her expression thoughtful, his sister moved back to the oven to check on the progress of the fragrant apple crumble she was baking. When she'd completed the task, she turned back to him with a frown, her blue eyes clearly reflecting both regret and concern about what he'd just shared. Having poured the wine, he handed her a glass.

'Thanks. Look, Jarrett, I'm so sorry about how I behaved when Sophia was here. I don't know what got into me. My only defence is that—as is my habit—I wanted to protect you. I know you're all grown up now, and you've achieved the kind of success that our parents probably dreamed of for us both when we were kids, but you're a rich, good-looking guy and I'm sorry to say that there are plenty of unscrupulous women out there who wouldn't hesitate to take advantage of you.'

'Weren't you suggesting that *I* was the unscrupulous one—trying to get to know her in order to persuade her to sell the house?'

'Yes, but that was before—'

In no mood to be either diplomatic or polite, Jarrett exploded. 'Before *what*? For your information Sophia Markham is a million miles away from the kind of woman you think she is. If you knew what she'd survived then you wouldn't be so quick to imagine that she's some kind of mercenary man-eater!'

Dragging his fingers impatiently through his hair, he strode across the room and back again in a bid to try and dispel the red mist of fury that had stealthily crept up on him. When he returned to stand in front of his sister once more, much to his indignation he saw that she hadn't taken his outburst at all seriously—instead, she was smiling...*smiling*, for goodness' sake!

'You're in love with her, aren't you?' she commented in wonder. 'That's what I was going to say to you...that I realised you didn't just want to get to know her to purchase the house. The real reason was because you'd fallen in love.'

Jarrett stared at her in open-mouthed surprise. Then he clamped his teeth together and made a dismissive jerk of his head. *But there was no point in denying it*. He knew that there were times when he could be obtuse, but this wasn't one of them. All Beth had done was put a name to the alternately painful and exhilarating intensity of the feelings he had for Sophia. But somehow to hear it declared out loud like that made it all the more real and incontrovertible.

'Yes, I am...' Now it was his turn to express his wonder.

Immediately closing the gap between them, Beth flung her arms around him for the second time that evening. 'I'm so happy for you. Honestly

I am. Have you told her? Does she feel the same? If she doesn't then I want to know why!'

Lightly fastening his hands round her slim upper arms, he gave her a rueful smile. 'The answer to whether she feels the same is I don't know. But I do know that she's the only woman I've ever loved—and the only woman I ever *will* love.'

'And have you told her that?'

He sighed. 'We're taking a break from seeing each other at the moment.'

'You are?'

'She has some things she needs to deal with… baggage from the past that still haunts her—' He broke off from what he'd been going to say to take in a deep steadying breath. 'She's had the most horrendous time of it. That's all I'll say. I wanted to give her the time and space to take stock and find a way to put it behind her so that she can truly move on.'

'So you were the one that suggested you have a break?'

Doubt and guilt suddenly pulsed through him. 'Yes.'

'She must have been dreadfully upset if she cares about you as much as you do about her. It's my experience that most women want love and support when they're going through a hard time...not space,' Beth remarked astutely.

Dropping his hands from round her arms, Jarrett irritably spun away. 'You really know how to kick a guy when he's down, don't you?'

'I'm not trying to make you feel bad. I was only expressing an opinion.' Folding her arms, she nibbled thoughtfully at her full lower lip. 'And it doesn't mean that I'm right. Maybe Sophia *does* need a break to sort things out in her head. I don't know her well enough to comment.'

Impatiently rubbing his hand round his jaw, he sensed his heart constrict with sudden dread. 'What if she doesn't?' He frowned. 'What if she did prefer that I stay with her and show her how much I care instead of suggesting we take a break from seeing each other? What if I've done the completely wrong thing?'

'Go to her,' Beth advised gently. 'Go to her and tell her exactly what you've just told me...that you love her and want to be with her come what may. I guarantee she won't ask you to leave.'

'You can go in now,' the receptionist advised Sophia.

She rose from her seat in such haste that the glossy copy of *Tatler* slithered off her lap and fell to the floor. Flustered, with her heart throbbing like a drum, she quickly retrieved it and returned it to the polished table in the centre of the room. As she walked through the brass-handled mahogany door the receptionist held open for her she made sure she inhaled a good lungful of air to bolster her courage.

The man she'd come to see was standing with his back to her by the huge plate-glass window. Its only adornment was the plain net curtain that allowed a good portion of very welcome light to flood into what was otherwise a quite sombre room. Attired in an immaculate charcoal-grey pinstriped suit, he cut a tall, imposing figure. When he turned round to focus his hard berry-brown eyes on her Sophia's legs buckled a little…but *only* a little. His long face was much more lined and careworn than she remembered, she observed, and his mouth still curved down at the edges, denoting that he rarely ever smiled.

Lifting her chin, she met his forbiddingly stern countenance with an equally unwavering stare of her own. 'Hello, Sir Christopher,' she said coolly.

'You've led me a merry dance, young lady. I've scoured the country looking for you,' he answered irritably. 'You weren't using either your married or your maiden name according to my sources.' Nodding curtly towards the leather-backed chair in front of the desk he scowled. 'You had better sit down. I want to make sure you're listening very carefully when I say what I have to say.'

'What you have to say is neither here nor there. I haven't come to hear one of your lectures on my conduct, and neither have I come to hear you set down terms for our future association. As far as me and my son are concerned, there *isn't* going to be one.'

'You can't keep me from seeing my grandson.

If this is how you intend on proceeding then I will issue a court order immediately for his custody.'

'No, you won't.' Sophia's voice was almost chillingly calm. Coolly she brushed away a piece of lint that clung to her jacket sleeve. 'You won't do that, Sir Christopher, because if you do my lawyer will slap a writ on you for substantial damages on my behalf. Not only that, but tomorrow morning you'll find a very interesting and revealing article about you and your despicable son in your copy of *The Times*.'

'You're bluffing. You can't afford a lawyer. My son left you with—'

'Nothing?' Sophia suggested helpfully. 'You're absolutely right, of course. And *why* did he leave his widow and his son with nothing? I'll remind you. He left us destitute because he spent every penny that came his way on drink, drugs and any other seedy pursuit you care to mention. I even had to sell our home so that I could pay off the horrendous debts he'd accumulated. And of course that played right into your hands, didn't it? You didn't step in and offer to help pay his debts yourself, did you? Oh, no. Instead you arrogantly insisted that Charlie and I come and live with you, so that you could maintain control over us both. Do you know what, Sir Christopher? I'd rather drill nails in my knees and crawl along the ground in agony for the rest of my life than ever contemplate such a repellent thing! Your precious son was a vain, cruel man, who made my life hell from the moment he married me, and it's hardly a surprise when he had the example of such a man as yourself as his father.'

The barrister in front of her looked visibly shocked. His pale cheeks had turned quite florid and the veins in his temple throbbed warningly. Still standing, Sophia clenched her fists down by her sides so that her nails bit into her palms and refused to allow herself to be remotely intimidated.

'And if I *do* decide to press charges,' she continued, 'I have to tell you that I've kept the vile letters you wrote me when you were still my father-in-law, warning me that if I ever told anyone what your dear son was putting me and Charlie through the consequences would be *dire* indeed. I would guess that they would be evidence enough for me to bring a very strong case, wouldn't you? My lawyer thinks so. In fact, he can't wait for me to give him the go-ahead so that he can start proceedings against you.'

'Who *is* this damned lawyer you say you've hired? Give me his name.'

'I don't need to give you his name. At least not until I instruct him to bring a case. Suffice to say he's got an impressive record in dealing with similar cases of marital abuse from the wives of men in the public eye.'

'You damn little bitch!'

The man behind the desk was shaking so hard with fury that spittle flew out of his mouth along with the insult. Sophia did flinch then—but only because she was disgusted. 'You can call me any names you like, Sir Christopher, but frankly I'm immune to them. I'm standing up for myself after five sickening years of unbelievable cruelty meted out by you and your son. If you want to maintain the esteemed reputation you're so proud of, I suggest you think carefully about what you're going to do. When I leave here it will be to visit the office of my lawyer. Whether I instruct him to prosecute you or not depends on your signature to the agreement I've had him draw up for me. The first thing I want you to agree is that you will never make any attempt, either now or in the future, to take Charlie away from me, or to interfere in his life or mine. If he chooses to see you when he's grown up, then that will be up to him. Do you want to read the document, or do I simply tell my lawyer to go ahead and press charges?'

In answer the barrister took the perfectly ironed handkerchief from his pocket and mopped the beads of sweat gathering on his face. He slumped down into his throne-like chair behind the desk with a defeated sigh the like of which Sophia had never heard him emit before in the entire time she'd known him.

CHAPTER ELEVEN

THE apple pie she'd made sat cooling on the sill by the open kitchen window. A tantalising breeze stirred outside, reminding her that it was late spring and soon the longer days would come. But tonight even the dark of the evening seemed kind.

Sophia hugged herself. It had been many years since she'd felt content enough to contemplate nature without fear tainting her musings. Her daily life had been full of such unbearable hardships and challenges she hadn't allowed herself much time for hopes and dreams. It had been too bitter to think that they would never come true.

But today, after her late husband's father had signed the agreement she'd given him, Sophia was free. Free at last from the chains of a destructive relationship that had imprisoned her mind, body and spirit for too long. At last she could make plans for her and her son's future. Not only that, she could restore High Ridge Hall to the beauty it deserved—because Sir Christopher had made out a substantial cheque for damages to her and, as he'd gruffly added, 'So that my grandson can be taken care of in the manner in which he deserves.' It was probably the closest thing to an apology she would ever receive from that hard-hearted man.

Yet she wasn't quite as happy as she yearned to be.

It had only been three days since she'd seen Jarrett, but each day had felt more like a year without sight of his handsome face, twinkling blue eyes and the sound of his resonant deep voice. Just how long did he intend them to be apart? Had these past three days helped him conclude that because of her damaged past she just wasn't worth the stress and strain that a relationship with her might entail?

Not wanting to dwell on too many negatives, Sophia restlessly got up from her place by the table where she'd been sitting sipping her tea to move across to the open window and take a breath of the soft night air. Once there, she paused to admire the tantalisingly aromatic apple pie she'd made, with its perfect golden crust and delicate decoration of leaf-shaped pastry. Her sole reason for making it was so that she could take it over to Jarrett and ask him to reconsider his suggestion about them taking a break. She was also eager to share the good news of her triumph today.

But, glancing over at the kitchen clock, she saw that it was nearing nine in the evening. What if she'd left it too late for visiting or he wasn't there? What if he was out for the evening or still at his office? Even waiting until tomorrow for the chance to see him again was too much to be endured…

The harsh sound of the door-knocker suddenly filled the air, piercing her reflections. Scarcely pausing to think, she flew down the corridor, praying hard that by some miracle the caller was Jarrett.

To her joy…*it was*. He was wearing a black

cashmere coat over his stylish suit, and the spicy scent of his cologne mingled with the mild night air made Sophia's tummy flip. He looked simply wonderful.

Her first instinct was to immediately throw her arms around him so that she could feel the reassuring strength of his body against hers. She'd so yearned for the opportunity to do that again. But just then she saw what she thought was a flicker of doubt and maybe even reticence in his deep blue eyes, and she froze. In that interminably frightening moment Sophia wondered if he'd come to tell her that he was breaking their association off for good.

'Hi.' Her greeting was helplessly uncertain.

'Hi, yourself.' In the fading evening light Jarrett's unreserved smile was like the sun coming out. 'I know I suggested we should spend some time apart, but I'm afraid I've come to tell you that I just can't keep to my part of the agreement after all.'

'You can't?' She desperately wanted to smile

back at him, but it was hard to control the quiver in her lips. 'Why not?'

'Why not?' he echoed, ruefully shaking his head. 'Perhaps you'd better invite me in first so I can tell you.'

'Okay. Please come in, Mr Gaskill.'

'It will be my pleasure, Ms Markham.'

'Will you come into the kitchen with me first? I have a surprise waiting for you…*two*, in actual fact.' Confident now that she had nothing to fear, Sophia caught Jarrett's hand as she slammed the door shut behind them and guided him into the long dim hallway. The firmness of his grip as he curled his fingers round hers thrilled her right down to the marrow. 'Shut your eyes and don't peep,' she playfully instructed him as they stood on the threshold of the kitchen rendered cosily warm from her baking.

Jarrett obediently closed his eyes. 'Has Charlie come back home?'

'He's coming home tomorrow afternoon. Did you think that was the surprise?'

'I did,' he admitted. 'I've missed not seeing the little man.'

'You have?' Sophia could have kissed him for that.

'Yes, I have. Now, just how long do you intend to keep me in suspense before you give me my surprise? There's a seriously tantalising aroma in here, and it's making my mouth water.'

Retrieving the pie in its still warm dish from the windowsill, she set it carefully down on the table in front of him. 'You can open your eyes now.'

He gave a throaty chuckle when he saw the pie. 'You made this for me?'

Sophia's cheeks flushed with pleasure. 'I promised that I would—remember?'

He didn't reply straight away. Instead he slipped off his cashmere coat and laid it over the back of a ladder-backed chair. Then he turned round to her and circled her tiny waist with his big hands to impel her gently but firmly against him. 'Want to hear why I couldn't keep to my part of the deal?' he challenged.

With her heart thudding hard inside her chest, her glance locked joyfully with his, she answered softly, 'Yes, I do'

'I couldn't stay away because I love you, Sophia. I love you with everything in me that's good and noble and honourable, and I want to spend the rest of my life showing you just how much I adore you. I know that you probably need plenty of time and space to heal the pain of your past but I was hoping I could help you by being the one you turn to when things get rough. I don't want you to have to cope with your troubles on your own. I'll always do whatever I can to make your path a little easier, I promise.'

It wasn't easy to form a reply because her heart was full to overflowing with a great swell of love for him. In her wildest dreams Sophia had never imagined a man would ever say such wonderful things to her—and mean them. But she only had to see the truth and concern in Jarrett's eyes to know that his declaration was utterly genuine.

'I guarded my heart against you, you know,' she admitted softly, laying her hand over the lapel of his fine wool jacket and sensing the heat from his body that permeated it. 'But somehow…somehow you managed to storm all my defences and reach me. I think I'll spend the rest of my life being glad that you did. These past three days without you have felt like a prison sentence. Just in case you haven't already realised…I love you too.'

She heard the sharp intake of breath he emitted before he lowered his head and kissed her. His warm lips moved over hers with a kind of savage hunger that electrified her, and she responded with an equally voracious desire, her hands moving urgently over his hard male form as if she wanted to climb right inside him. It made her realise that the youthful fascination she'd once had for her husband was nothing but a short sharp breeze when compared to this urgent, quiet storm that tore through her whenever Jarrett was near.

Tearing at the buttons on his shirt to free them, she moved her hand inside the material so that she could feel the throb of his heartbeat and the warmth of his skin, even as he made a similar move and palmed her breast through her sweater. She released a ragged moan when his fingers teased and then pinched her nipple, a spear of scalding erotic heat flashing right through her core.

It became quickly evident that their urgent fumbling was not enough for either of them, but it was Jarrett who articulated his frustration first.

'We need a bed.' Breathing hard, he grinned as his gaze lit on her animated flushed face. 'I adore you, my angel, and will always treat you with the utmost respect, but that doesn't mean that I don't lust after you like crazy. Any time that I don't have you in my arms…in my *bed*… is wasted time as far as I'm concerned.'

'Well…' Sophia dimpled as she lovingly touched her hand to his cheek. 'Will *my* bed do for now, do you think?'

'That answer is music to my ears. But first I have a question to ask you.'

'Oh?' Already weak with anticipation of making love with him again, she tried hard to stem her impatience to head straight for the bedroom. 'What's that?'

'Will you marry me?'

'Are you serious, Jarrett?' The question drove away every other thought in her head. Now she wasn't just weak, she was breathless too.

'Haven't I just told you that I want to spend the rest of my life showing you how much I adore you? It stands to reason that I want to marry you, doesn't it? Besides, I need a good woman like you to make an honest man out of me.'

'You *are* an honest man—a good man I can trust…and they're two of the qualities I love about you the most.'

Beneath his lightly tanned skin he flushed a little. 'Thank you.'

'But marriage is a big step, Jarrett. Are you really sure you want to take it? And don't forget you'd be taking Charlie on as well as me.'

'It *is* a big step, my darling, and one I never contemplated until I met you. But now that I'm head over heels in love with you nothing else will do. And as for becoming stepfather to your fine little son…I'd be honoured.'

'That's a good answer. Go to the top of the class.' Sophia grinned. 'So your bachelor days will be well and truly over if we marry?'

'And I thank heaven for that. Haven't you guessed that you're the woman I've been waiting for most of my life? One look into those incredible eyes of yours and I was smitten. I can remember leaving you by the brook with Charlie in your arms, somehow knowing that my life would never be the same. Now, for God's sake, put me out of my misery and give me your answer,' he pleaded, and this time there was a real flicker of doubt in his eyes.

Not wanting him to suffer unnecessarily, Sophia stood up on tiptoe and planted a loving, lingering kiss on his lips. 'My answer is yes, Jarrett. I *will* marry you. I'm sure there are plenty of people who would probably advise me to take longer to think about it after my first marriage— but I honestly don't think I have anything to fear this time round. I feel absolutely certain that I'm meant to be with you, and I'd be honoured to be your wife.'

Cupping her jaw, Jarrett moved the pad of his thumb across her naked mouth to tenderly trace her lips. 'That's settled, then.'

It was the most understated yet most profound response Sophia could have wished for, because she easily detected the catch in his voice that told her just how much her agreement meant to him.

'Remember I told you that I had two surprises?' she reminded him, suddenly anxious to share the immensity and importance of her trip to London earlier that day. 'Do you want me to tell you about the second one?'

Gently, she extricated herself from his warm embrace so that she could think straight and breathe more easily. She was apt to feel too intoxicated to do either with ease when she was in his arms.

'Go on.' He was shrugging off his suit jacket as he spoke and, briefly turning to the chair where he'd left his coat, he hooked the jacket over a corner. Then he removed his tie.

Sophia's mouth went dry. The collar and a good part of the top of his shirt were already partially undone where she'd torn at the buttons, giving her a tantalising glimpse of the fine curling dark hairs on his chest, and as he stripped away the corporate persona he wore for work he looked very warrior-like, she thought—like a seasoned campaigner home from the wars whose most urgent need was to bed his woman and bed her *soon*.

Heat suffusing her, she let her tongue nervously moisten her lips. 'I took your advice and rang that lawyer friend of yours,' she declared, her words spilling out in an anxious rush.

When Jarrett received this information in silence, standing perfectly still as if his every sense was on high alert, she breathed in deeply before continuing.

'He more or less told me to come and see him straight away. He postponed a couple of other appointments, because he knew that you'd asked him for help on my behalf.' Tendering a lopsided smile, she carried on. 'So I went up to London, and when I gave him a full account of my story he was really helpful and supportive…just like you said he'd be. He told me I had a practically cast-iron case against Sir Christopher. I was overwhelmed that he believed me and didn't suggest I was making it up. I suppose I'd worried about that. Anyhow, before I made any decision to prosecute I rang Sir Christopher's office and arranged to see him too.'

Jarrett frowned deeply, as if expecting to hear the worst, but nevertheless he held his tongue and remained silent.

'You would have been proud of me. For the first time in all the years that I've known him I stood up to him and refused to be intimidated or made to feel small. He didn't expect that. I think he thought that I'd come to him hoping for a handout and to admit that I had been wrong to run away. I can't tell you how incredible it made me feel to disappoint him. But the most empowering thing of all was being able to say at last exactly how I felt about his son's mistreatment of me as well as his own. I told him that if he didn't stop harassing me and threatening to take Charlie away then I'd give a statement to *The Times* exposing his family's cruelty. He was shocked that I'd even *dared* to threaten such a thing. Bullies never expect their prey to fight back, do they? I could see that he was seriously rattled...*scared*, even. In that moment it was as though a cold heavy stone had been rolled away from inside my heart and I was free to be myself again...to stand up for my rights and fear no one.'

'That was a truly brave thing you did, confronting him like that. And I *am* proud of you, Sophia...immensely proud. So what happened after you threatened him with taking your story to the newspapers?'

Sophia's smile was wide. 'He signed the agreement that your lawyer friend helped me compose, stating that he wasn't to pursue any association with me or Charlie ever again. At the end of the day an egotistical man like him was never going to risk his reputation or have a bad word said in public about his son...even though he was such a bastard. Everything was conducted in a professional manner, and his signature was witnessed and countersigned by a solicitor who practises in an office down the hall. When the man was curious as to the content of the document Sir Christopher brushed him off, telling him it was just a "small' family matter" that he needed to attend to. I have a copy of the agreement for myself, and I took a second one back to your lawyer friend for him to keep in his records before I came home.'

'That was a good move.'

'Thank you so much for speaking to him about me. I felt much more secure talking to someone that you personally know and recommended.'

'It was my pleasure to help you, sweetheart, and you don't need to thank me.'

'Oh, but I do! In the short time that I've known you you've done so much for me, Jarrett, and I want you to know that I appreciate it and take nothing for granted.'

'Do you think Charlie will ever want to see his grandfather again?'

She shrugged. 'If he wants to make contact

when he's grown up, then that will be entirely down to him. Anyway, the meeting ended with him writing me a substantial cheque for damages… Hush money, I think they call it in the movies. Anyway, the amount was more or less what I sold my house for to meet Tom's debts. And to be honest—without taking him to court—it was a bonus I didn't expect.'

'A bonus, you call it?' Jarrett scowled fiercely. 'It was the least he could bloody well do after the hell he and his son put you through!'

'But *he's* the one in hell now, when you think about it. Not only has he lost his only son, but his grandson too. I'm sure as he gets older—especially if he continues living alone—he'll reflect more and more on both losses and bitterly regret it. I genuinely feel sorry for him.'

'You are one in a million—you know that?' Wrapping his arms around her, Jarrett gazed tenderly down into her eyes. 'I don't think there are many people that would be so quick to feel pity for someone who'd mistreated them as badly as you've been mistreated.'

'I can feel pity for him because he's now firmly in my past and no longer features in my present. The same goes for Tom.' Anchoring her arms more firmly round his waist, Sophia breathed out a contented sigh.

'So, after your hard-won triumph, you're in the mood to celebrate, I take it?'

'Yes, I am. I tell you what—I'll make us a nice cup of tea and cut us both a slice of that pie I made you. How about that?' she replied, pretending she didn't understand the hopeful and lascivious glint in his eye.

'Tempting as it sounds…that's *not* how I want to help you celebrate.' Without further preamble, Jarrett tipped her up into his arms, and he did indeed put her in mind of a warrior again, with the fiercely purposeful expression he wore on his handsome sculpted face. 'I have something much more satisfying in mind than apple pie… delicious as I'm sure it undoubtedly is.'

'Are you perhaps suggesting that I show you where my bed is located?'

'Your ability to read minds is seriously impressive, Ms Markham,' he said wryly. And without further ado he followed Sophia's happily voiced directions to her bedroom along the hall...

Jarrett propped himself up on his elbow to study his lover's gently slumbering form. In the soft glow of the lamp he saw that one slender arm was flung out over the rumpled red and cream quilt, and her long chestnut hair flowed unhindered down her back like a rippling fire-lit river.

Freed from the dark history that had entrapped her spirit for so long, she'd lost any inhibitions she might have had to fully express her desire, and their passionate lovemaking on this night would be an experience he would never forget. Even now, when a good hour had passed since their rapturous union, his body still throbbed. He just about suppressed a groan at the memory. Never in his thirty-six years had Jarrett guessed or even *imagined* that loving a woman with all his heart could be so ecstatic...could bring him more joy and satisfaction than anything he'd ever experienced before. More wondrous still was the pride and delight he felt that Sophia had agreed to become his wife.

He was so grateful to his sister that she'd urged him to go to her tonight. There was no doubt in his mind that she would be over the moon at the outcome.

Having spent a long time privately yearning to experience the sense of truly coming home to a woman who loved him as deeply as he loved her, now that he'd incredibly got what he'd wished for he vowed passionately to himself that he would guard and protect Sophia with his life. And at the same time he would always give her the freedom and encouragement to do whatever made her happy.

His musings turned to her son Charlie. A thrill of pride shot through him when he thought about becoming his stepfather. After the boy's natural father had mentally abused him, and let him down so badly, Jarrett would make it his mission to help replace his hurtful memories of the past with much more loving and positive ones. He would show him what a difference it could make to his life to have a man who really cared about him and his mother as his parent.

Stirring, Sophia turned onto her back, blinking up at him with quizzical green eyes. 'Can't you sleep?'

'Not really.'

'Why?' She was immediately concerned.

'I'm just too happy to go to sleep, I guess. I was just sitting here admiring you, and thinking that I've never seen you look so relaxed and at peace.' Lifting her hand, he tenderly pressed his lips to the centre of her palm. Coming into contact with her matchless silken skin again, he sensed the blood in his veins quicken and heat.

Her lips split into a grin. 'Well, I've honestly never *felt* this relaxed or at peace before...I suppose that's why. Plus I'm basking in the glow of our wild and passionate lovemaking, don't you know?'

Turning towards him, she trailed her fingers down over his bare chest, letting them glance provocatively against the skin an inch or two below his belly button.

Jarrett sensed himself instantly harden. 'You're playing with fire, woman,' he growled, then threw back the rumpled quilt and straddled her.

Her teasing grin instantly vanished. Instead her glance became much more focused, and her pupils turned inky jet with desire.

'And things are about to get even hotter,' he told her huskily, 'because that was only the warm-up.'

'Really?'

'Yes…*really*.' He entered her with one smooth powerful stroke, and was gratified to hear her whimper of pleasure.

After that, Jarrett had no further need or desire to talk any further…

EPILOGUE

One year later...

IT HAD been a long time since the gardens at High Ridge had appeared so beautiful. It had been hard work restoring it, but surveying it today, in the bright sunshine, Sophia thought it had been more than worth every bit of toil and sweat she and Jarrett had expended. Believing that it was important for a sense of pride and achievement to have a personal input into the restoration of the gardens and the house, and not just hire professionals to come in and do the job, together she and Jarrett had tended to the myriad of plants and flowers with every spare moment they had, as well as implementing the ongoing work on the major restoration of both the interior and exterior of the house.

Along with the very professional darkroom she'd dreamed of, so far they had a bathroom and spa to die for, newly designed bedrooms, and a drawing room with several seriously comfortable and beautiful sofas and armchairs. And having developed a sentimental fondness for her great aunt Mary's rickety old couch, after initially storing it in one of the unused bedrooms Sophia had recently had it despatched to a professional upholsterer's where it was being restored.

Since they had married last year, and Jarrett had moved in with her, they had both become keen to transform the genteel old house into their own vision of a beautiful family home they could be proud of. But even with that aim firmly in mind they both knew what the most important values that made a real home were *love and family*. And today they had invited their friends and family to help them celebrate not only their first wedding anniversary and the restoration of the gardens but the news that they were most excited about of all…that she and Jarrett were expecting their first child together.

'One fresh apple juice, made with apples from our very own orchard, for the ravishingly beautiful Mrs Gaskill!'

Sophia called a halt to her surveying of the gardens from the newly installed drawing room patio with a start, and spun round to find her husband, casually attired in jeans and a black roll-necked sweater and looking more handsome than ever, theatrically brandishing an antique silver salver with a single glass of juice on it.

'Now, that's what I call service,' she said, smiling and lifted it off the tray.

'I aim to please,' he replied with a wink, setting down the salver on a side table and returning to lightly lay his hands either side of her waist. 'By the way, I love what you're wearing today.'

She had on a vintage white dress, and had teamed it with a pretty daffodil-yellow ribbed cardigan. She had to admit she did indeed feel pretty in the outfit. Perhaps it was because of the news she was all but bursting to share with their family and friends? It didn't matter. All Sophia knew was that she was happier than she'd ever been in her life. The harsh life that she'd led with Tom Abingdon no longer haunted her as much as it had used to. Her only sadness was that her dad couldn't be there to witness her joy.

'You always know just what to say to make me feel good,' she remarked, and received a long, lingering kiss from Jarrett in return.

'If I do,' he replied, lifting his head, 'it's only because when I look at you I can't help but speak from the heart.'

'Well, you look pretty good yourself, if you don't mind my saying so. I really like you in that black sweater. Makes you look vaguely mysterious…sexy too. Your sister hasn't invited any of her predatory friends to our little party, has she?'

'She wouldn't dare. In any case, even if she has I wouldn't notice them. Not when I'm married to the loveliest and most alluring woman in the world.'

Sophia emitted a soft groan. 'Stop saying such provocative things or I'll be waiting for everyone to go just so that we can get to bed.'

Her husband grinned with pleasure. 'Once

Charlie's asleep—going by our record so far—that will be our first destination anyway. Are you looking forward to seeing your brother and his troupe today?'

'Very much so!'

'Do you think he'll be pleased about the baby?'

'Of course he will, my darling. He'll be over-joyed. How many times has he told us that we ought to have a brood of kids? Five or six at the very least! Talking of kids…do you know where Charlie is? I left him in the kitchen eating chocolate ice cream just ten minutes ago, and I'll probably have to get him to change his shirt and jeans before our visitors get here because no doubt they're covered in the stuff by now.'

'He wasn't in the kitchen when I poured your drink a minute ago.'

'Then where is—?'

Before Sophia had finished speaking the boy in question tore into the room and out onto the patio, pursued by the rapidly growing light cream Labrador puppy that Jarrett had adopted for him on the day they'd got married. Right now, both boy and dog wore the evidence of the chocolate ice-cream on their faces and on their bodies—and in Charlie's case all over his previously clean white shirt and jeans.

'What on earth—?'

'Sorry, Mum, but Sam wanted to share my ice cream and I wanted him to have some. I couldn't be mean and not give him any, could I?' Spinning round, her small son gazed hopefully up at Jarrett, as if searching for an ally. 'I'm right, Dad, aren't I?'

Jarrett's colour visibly rose beneath his cleanly shaved jaw and Sophia's heart turned over, because she knew how much it meant to him to hear Charlie refer to him as 'Dad'. She almost held her breath as she waited for him to respond.

'Yes, son…you are right. I agree,' he answered, and when his eyes next met hers they had never seemed more crystal blue…like the finest-cut diamonds glinting in the sun.

Her heart swelled with love and pride for the two men that meant the most to her in the world…

* * * * *

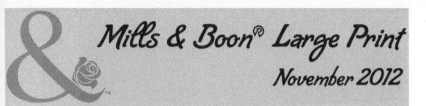

Mills & Boon® Large Print
November 2012

THE SECRETS SHE CARRIED
Lynne Graham

TO LOVE, HONOUR AND BETRAY
Jennie Lucas

HEART OF A DESERT WARRIOR
Lucy Monroe

UNNOTICED AND UNTOUCHED
Lynn Raye Harris

ARGENTINIAN IN THE OUTBACK
Margaret Way

THE SHEIKH'S JEWEL
Melissa James

THE REBEL RANCHER
Donna Alward

ALWAYS THE BEST MAN
Fiona Harper

A ROYAL WORLD APART
Maisey Yates

DISTRACTED BY HER VIRTUE
Maggie Cox

THE COUNT'S PRIZE
Christina Hollis

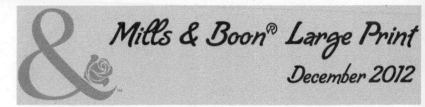

Mills & Boon® Large Print
December 2012

CONTRACT WITH CONSEQUENCES
Miranda Lee

THE SHEIKH'S LAST GAMBLE
Trish Morey

THE MAN SHE SHOULDN'T CRAVE
Lucy Ellis

THE GIRL HE'D OVERLOOKED
Cathy Williams

MR RIGHT, NEXT DOOR!
Barbara Wallace

THE COWBOY COMES HOME
Patricia Thayer

THE RANCHER'S HOUSEKEEPER
Rebecca Winters

HER OUTBACK RESCUER
Marion Lennox

A TAINTED BEAUTY
Sharon Kendrick

ONE NIGHT WITH THE ENEMY
Abby Green

THE DANGEROUS JACOB WILDE
Sandra Marton

1112 Rom LP